CONTENTS

In memory of
my dear friend
Jill Bowles
(1948 – 2004)

Dedicated to my lovely family
I adore you & am so proud of you all

Towards The Hills

A Spiritual Journey
From Darkness into the Light and
I Waited Patiently
An Anthology of Encouragement

By

Julie Robas

MAPLE
PUBLISHERS

Towards The Hills

Author: Julie Robas

Copyright © Julie Robas (2025)

The right of Julie Robas to be identified as author of this work has been asserted by the author in accordance with section 77 and 78 of the Copyright, Designs and Patents Act 1988.

First Published in 2025

ISBN 978-1-83538-468-8 (Paperback)
978-1-83538-469-5 (Hardback)
978-1-83538-470-1 (E-Book)

Cover Design and Book Layout by:
White Magic Studios
www.whitemagicstudios.co.uk

Published by:
Maple Publishers
Fairbourne Drive, Atterbury,
Milton Keynes,
MK10 9RG, UK
www.maplepublishers.com

A CIP catalogue record for this title is available from the British Library.

O God, wherever I go today, help me to leave heartprints! Heartprints of compassion, understanding, and love. Heartprints of kindness and genuine concern. May my heart touch a lonely neighbour or runaway daughter or anxious mother or even an aged grandfather. Send me out today to leave heartprints. And if someone should say, 'I felt your touch,' may that one sense Your love touching through me.

Prayer by unknown author

Acknowledgements

While every effort has been made to contact the copyright holders of material used in this book, this has not always been successful. Full acknowledgement will gladly be made in future editions.

We gratefully acknowledge the following, extracts from which appear in this book:

William Horwood, *The Boy With No Shoes*

Fiona Castle, *Rainbows Through the Rain*

Michael J. Fox, *Lucky Man*

Philip Yancey, *What's So Amazing About Grace?*

Denyse Devlin, *The Catalpa Tree*, Penguin Books

A.T. Pierson, *George Müller of Bristol*

Frank Topping, *Lord of My Days*

Christopher Reeve, *Nothing Is Impossible*

The following are also gratefully acknowledged:

'Father of life, draw me closer' (Let the peace of God reign)

Copyright © 1995 Darlene Zschech/Hillsongs Australia/ Kingsway's Thankyou Music, PO Box 75, Eastbourne, East Sussex BN23 6NW, UK.

'The Heart of Worship'

Copyright © 1997 Matt Redman, Thankyou Music/MCPS

'You Are My Anchor'

Copyright © 2001 Stuart Townend, Thankyou Music (Admin by Kingsway Music)

'The Voice of Hope'

Copyright ©2002 Lara Martin, Thankyou Music (Admin by Kingsway Music)

'Jesus Be The Centre'

Copyright © 1999 Michael Frye, Vineyard Songs (UK/Eire)/ Copycare

'In Christ Alone'

© 2001 Stuart Townend & Keith Getty, Thankyou Music/MCPS

'The Potter's House'

Sung by Tramaine Hawkins

Great Women of Gospel, EMI Gospel (copyright info)

'I Am a New Creation'

Words and music: David Bilbrough

Copyright © 1983, Thankyou Music (Admin by Kingsway Music)

PO Box 75, Eastbourne, East Sussex BN23 6NW, UK

Introduction

If I were to sum it up in a few words, I would describe depression as being a cancer of the soul. The symptoms are many and I know that the ones I suffered from are classic – debilitating tiredness and lethargy, where your limbs feel like lead and you feel as if your blood is only sluggishly trickling through your veins. I used to feel like I was carrying around a leaden blackness in my chest – I knew only too well what the phrase "heavy-hearted" meant. My mind, too, was filled with darkness. Different events in my life were compartmented in my memory and for each event there was an image in my mind, like a computer desktop full of icons, and all of them were black.

This depression was often combined with anxiety. Ongoing stresses throughout the years had caused me to develop the habit of being anxious. I had difficulty concentrating, my thoughts were tormented and I longed to be able to switch my mind off. Sometimes I would be driving along and would suddenly be seized with an overwhelming urge to squeeze my foot down on the accelerator. I could vividly envisage the car smashing into a lamp post and I would feel a momentary surge of release at the promise of oblivion this violent impact would bring; the beautiful numbness almost tangible. I would immediately be overcome with feelings of guilt and remorse for these thoughts, when I had family who loved me and family to care for.

I would often find myself trapped in this negative and unproductive thought cycle of suicidal schemes followed by guilt, heart ache at the thought of leaving loved ones behind and a paralysing fear of death. Like *Ol' Man River* I was tired of living but scared of dying. I wanted to live to take care of my family but I wanted the painful feelings to come to an end.

All I wanted to do was sleep, although at times sleep eluded me, and I had bad dreams – often bloody and violent dreams that were so vivid and real that I would wake up feeling shaken and disturbed and it would take some time for this feeling to subside.

I dreaded each day, I struggled to get out of bed every morning and especially on the weekends when I didn't have to get up to take the kids to school or go to work. I could never commit or get involved in things because I knew I couldn't be relied on.

I have always been a dreamer and love nothing more than to sit curled up in my favourite armchair and gaze out into the back garden, at the sky, the trees, the flowers and the birds but when I was experiencing one of my 'downers' I felt detached from everything; surroundings and people. I had the sensation that I was seeing and hearing things from a great distance and if I was looking out at the garden I would feel incapable of absorbing the beauty of a view that would normally fill me with solace and peace.

Julie Robas

28 November 2006

PART ONE

Towards The Hills

A Spiritual Journey from Darkness into the Light

I said to the man who stood at the gate of the Year, "Give me a light that

I may tread safely into the unknown." And he replied, "Go out into the darkness and put your hand into the Hand of God. That shall be to you better than light and safer than a known way!"

So I went forth and finding the Hand of God, trod gladly into the night. And He led me towards the hills and the breaking of day in the lone east.

Minnie Louise Haskins (1875 – 1957)

Chapter One

"Give me a light that I may tread safely into the unknown..."

As I wandered up the road to my grandparents' house in West Sussex, deep in thought, a long row of terraced houses to my right and the railway tracks and Littlehampton railway station to my left, I looked down at my feet as they moved one in front of the other and pictured the different occasions over the years that I had traipsed up this very road - with my children, before my grandparents had passed away; during my teens, when I had lived in England in the late seventies and early eighties; at the age of ten, when we had come over from Rhodesia for a holiday; toddling along at the age of three, before we immigrated to Africa and - to complete the reverse metamorphosis from adulthood to youth - being pushed in my pram as a baby, perhaps by my mother or grandmother. I had moved around from place to place over the years and this scene, the cry of the gulls audible as they flew over the nearby estuary and my head filled with the smell of the sea, was about the only setting that was truly familiar to me - my paternal grandparents and their home being one source of stability in my life. I reached the house, turned around and wandered back down the road to where the car was parked, only briefly glancing at the unfamiliar curtains now hanging in the windows, as I passed by.

My mother was born out of wedlock during the Second World War. Her mother died when she was eight years old and the man she knew to be her father passed away also, when she was fourteen. Stories of her childhood are fragmented but it seems that it was a grim time for her, apparently when her mother died a relative swooped through the house and removed all her mother's possessions – the only thing my mother was able to retrieve was an old glove. Mum also told us that after her mother died she often went hungry and on one occasion, when she was sent on an errand to buy meat at the butcher, she said she ate the raw mince on the way home.

During her late teens she met my father, as they moved in the same social circle, who used to play the trumpet at the dance halls on a Saturday night and my mother used to sing. In 1961 my mother found out that she was pregnant. At that time British people could sail out to Australia for £10 on the condition that they stayed a minimum of two years. This was to increase the labour force which had been depleted during the Second World War. My mum and dad got married before my mum began to show and without telling family of the pregnancy they sailed out to Australia, initially living in Sydney and then moving on to Hobart, Tasmania where my sister was born on 24th March, 1962. My mother felt ill-equipped emotionally to look after a baby and so my dad remorsefully and reluctantly agreed to give my sister up for adoption – a decision he has always regretted. Even in the early days of their marriage, while my mother was pregnant with my sister, her unstable character began to reveal itself when she began to get involved with other men.

Happy though mum was to put as much distance between herself and her unhappy past in England as possible, she soon tired of Australia and as soon as their obligatory two years were up they set sail for Canada. After just a few months there mum found out that she was expecting again. Dad, who was a printer by trade, was experiencing difficulty in finding work and with a child on the way they decided it was best to return to England for the impending birth. In Zachary Merton Hospital, just outside of Littlehampton, I was born on 23rd April, 1964. For the first three years of my life we moved from place to place, wherever dad could find work, until 1967 when we immigrated to, what was then, Salisbury, Rhodesia. Two of my father's brothers had immigrated there with their families and had recommended that my father do the same. From the day my mother set foot on Rhodesian soil she fell in love with the place - its beautiful sunny skies, its laid back way of life and its friendly folk - and my father did too. Over a period of time the warm, balmy weather cured him of his asthma, which he had suffered badly from in his youth. He often recounted stories of drab days, during the war years, shuffling off to school with his three brothers in the cold and the rain, his nose streaming with only a sopping wet rag to wipe it on, his toes all pinched and painful in boots that were too small for him and also of long hours spent chewing apathetically on food that appeared to him, with his constantly blocked nose, absolutely tasteless.

I've been told that I was a very quiet and contented baby. I'd sit propped up with cushions in the corner of an armchair happily sucking my thumb and surveying the scene before me. When I grew older I often liked to curl up in large cardboard boxes and I would take everything out of the bottom of my bedroom cupboard and climb inside with my comforter blanket and my toy piano. I also used to spend long hours sitting on my swing, making up little songs – the motion of the swing seeming to release my whimsical little spirit and what with mum constantly humming and singing and dad whistling, playing the trumpet and listening to jazz, music has always been a great part of my life.

I didn't have much company and I can't remember whether or not I was lonely. I think I was happy enough with my own company and when I learned to ride my bike I gained a little independence, cycling to school and visiting a couple of nearby friends. I remember that my grandparents came out to Rhodesia to stay with us for a few weeks around that time. Later, my Grandmother would often tell the story of how she was busy scrubbing my face, neck and ears in the bath one evening when I piped up, in shrill little voice, "Mind my ear 'oles Gran!"

However, I grew to be timid and excruciatingly shy. As I grew older I became an avid reader and would absolutely devour books in a range of subjects, anything from Homer to horror or Asimov to "Famous Five". I don't have many childhood memories of either of my parents, possibly because I spent so much time tinkering around on my own or, later on, immersed in my world of books. Cycling, also, became a passion and, again, this was something that I mostly did alone. Out on the long straight Rhodesian roads I would become one with my surroundings. My inhibitions cast aside, as I absorbed the sun, the sky, the dust, the dry grass and the intoxicating smell of the eucalyptus trees, I would stand on the pedals of my bike and pedal furiously, my hair streaming back (or so I liked to think) in the wind. Out on dirt tracks, the dryness of the surrounding bush almost tangible, I would swoop and dive, throwing myself with complete abandon down ditches and up the other side, dodging in and out of trees, slipping and sliding in the dust and gravel.

Our family led a quiet sort of life. My parents had a few friends whom I remember visiting at times. We quite often visited the nearby drive-in on a Saturday night, and there I was introduced to the world of Disney – Snow White and the Seven Dwarfs, Chitty Chitty Bang Bang, Bedknobs and Broomsticks.

We didn't see much of family so I don't have memories of family times or time spent with my cousins. My mother was not easy-going and never seemed able to get on with them and that combined with the fact that, later on, our faith made us different to them eventually caused us to stop seeing each other altogether.

In the last house we lived in, in Rhodesia (in eleven years we had moved six times), mum fell out with our next door neighbour and I remember one instance where the two of them paced to and fro, with the fence between the two properties mercifully separating them, like a pair of hounds, snarling at each other.

There were noticeable contradictions in my mother's nature. She could be wonderfully warm and friendly with an infectious laugh and I remember times when she and dad used to joke around, my father having a dry sense of humour, and mum would laugh until tears ran down her face. On the other hand, though, she could be unstable, erratic and headstrong. When she got angry she took on the nature of a cat and you daren't go near her. Her eyes would take on a cold and steely glint that made me feel edgy. I remember many an occasion when poor old dad got coerced into doing things that he was really loathe to do and which, sure enough, he really regretted but mum was not someone you could say 'no' to. Although she worked when I was little, she never seemed to be able to hold a job down for long – as far as I can understand the problem was that she fell out with people very easily. My parents' relationship was never easy and as I grew older I became very aware of that fact. The fact, also, that they might divorce at any time felt like a threat that was constantly hanging over me, making me feel anxious. My father used to talk to me sometimes, even to the point of confiding in me to a certain extent and I think this was because I was mature for my age and easy to talk to, unlike my mother. Overall, though, the situation caused me to become very serious-minded for a young girl and deep and intense conversations were the norm.

When I was little, in my deepest, darkest memory, I remember being aware of the presence of another man who I think was one of my mother's male-friends.

What held my parents together was, I think, the fact that dad loved her – pure and simple. I remember my father telling me once that when mum walked into a room full of people and her eyes settled on yours she made you feel like you were the only person in the room. Or if they were shopping in town and my father saw the familiar figure of my mother walking towards him in the street he would be filled with warmth towards her.

When I was eight years old we started attending church and this is where I met my husband to be and his family. This was the happiest period of my childhood. Living by biblical principles under the positive influence of church friends acted as a stabiliser for my family and into this more peaceful environment my brother was born. I was by this time eleven years old. I remember on the way home from the nursing home, sitting in the back of our old blue Citröen with my newborn brother in my arms, crying with happiness for the first time in my life. However, this initial response was severely put to the test with the many sleepless nights that followed and as I was made responsible for looking after him much of the time, changing his nappies and taking him out for walks while mum rested in the afternoons I did, at times, feel more than a little resentful. The noise of the wheels of his push chair rattling along the bumpy roads was mortifying as it seemed to echo all around the neighbourhood.

On the whole though, he was quite a cute little character. It used to amuse me how he would get around the garden on his first set of wheels, his baby walker. We had a large garden, about a square acre, with a circular dirt driveway, a lawn of kikuyu grass, lots of trees including fruit trees and blazing bougainvillea bushes and flower beds filled with cannas, dahlias, poinsettias, hibiscus, red-hot pokers and marigolds. My brother used to fling himself around the garden in his walker like a racing driver and when he encountered the hosepipe lying across his path he would lift the whole frame like a lady lifting her skirt, daintily step over it, slam the walker down on the other side, and then off he would go again in a cloud of dust.

My parents became close friends with my husband's parents, their personalities seemed to complement each other, my dad and his mum being calm and quiet and his dad and my mum being more boisterous, and we ended up spending most weekends in each other's company. As soon as we arrived at the respective house us kids would disappear to play together while our parents settled down to chat and games of canasta. When they came to our house on a Sunday afternoon we kids would often loll around on a blanket spread out on the lawn listening to "Forces Requests" on my radio. This was a programme where pop songs were played, and messages from family read out, to the soldiers who were away fighting in the Rhodesian bush war.

During my early teens, when I began to develop thoughts and opinions contrary to my mother's, she and I began to clash. I remember asking her for something trivial, once, and she rounded on me saying "Don't ever ask me for anything! I know what you need." But as time went by she clearly proved to have the attitude "I never had anything so why should you?" While many of my peers were fashionably dressed I had very little in the way of clothing, mum cut my hair and I went to high school with pigtails of different lengths and my brown lace up school shoes were at least two sizes too big for me (so I wouldn't grow out of them too soon, mum said, trouble was I never grew into them). They felt so big that I was sure that if I was coming around a corner you'd see my feet first. The end result of all this was that I went from being excruciatingly shy to excruciatingly self-conscious. I also began to realise that mum was very jealous of my father's relationship with me and, eventually, if dad ever bought me anything my mother would get angry.

By 1978 the Rhodesian bush war had been going on for some time and, like my friends' fathers mine was being called up to do stretches in the army. All around us we were hearing stories of family members who were being killed in service. It felt too close to home. Very suddenly my parents decided to pack up and move back to England and within a short space of time we sold up our home and left for England with just our suitcases. The Church we attended was an international organisation and had its own printing establishment in St. Albans, England. My father was offered a job there and we moved temporarily into church accommodation until we purchased our own home.

Here began the downward spiral for my family. I, who had at first looked forward to coming to England, suddenly woke up and realised that I'd left behind all that was familiar to me including my friends and boyfriend, and that I was alone and in a completely foreign environment and climate. When we moved into our house, although people from the church in England had been very kind and given us a house full of furniture, it was nevertheless a hodgepodge, all second-hand and nothing matched. It all seemed very drab. My mother was back in the country she dreaded and although she tried, she found it very hard to settle in and my father started doing shift work, working long and anti-social hours.

After I'd been at my new high-school for a short while I made one close friend and things became easier. I read as much as ever and I spent a lot of time out on my bike. In summertime when the days were long and hot I would spend whole days out cycling around the English country lanes and through the little villages, stopping off here and there to sit and daydream on a sunny little bench in a peaceful churchyard.

At home, though, things were starting to fall apart. The arguments got progressively worse and my mother's mental instability began to surface, her behaviour becoming more and more erratic as well as abusive. She seemed unable to control herself. As home life became more turbulent, I began to find school a means of escape but would, at times, arrive there in an emotional state. I spent more and more time at my friend's house and her family became a source of stability for me. Her parents were divorced and her mother was living with a partner. My friend missed her father and often seemed to struggle with her feelings about the divorce, so we had mutual woes but we also shared the same zany sense of humour and we had a lot of fun. My boyfriend and I also kept in contact with each other. By this time he had left home and joined the British South African Police.

My father began giving me two pounds a week pocket money and I saved up and bought my own clothes. The last clothes my mother bought me was my English school uniform when I was fourteen. When I turned sixteen I found a Saturday job, working at a bookshop in town, and the extra cash was a great help.

With my mother's extreme mood swings she could be warm and happy one minute and then her personality was magnetic and I would find myself automatically drawn towards her. In these moments I would happily chatter away to her and even confide in her, but then the next minute her mood would change and she would end up twisting things that I'd told her confidentially and throwing them back in my face. Eventually I became distrustful and I learned to keep to myself, but I found it hard having to consciously resist her because all I wanted was her warmth. Despite everything, like my father, I loved her. She was my mother and all I wanted was to be close to her.

My mother once told me that if she had had a mother she would never have taken her for granted and she would not be convinced otherwise. Fortunately I've witnessed how fraught relationships between teenagers and parents, in many cases, smooth themselves out as years go by. When I had my own children I knew to be tolerant and wait for the not so easy years to blow over, but my mother didn't seem to have that kind of vision and reacted like things were never going to change for the better between us.

Eventually it got to the point where there was constant tension in our home. My mother really started to go off the rails and it was clear that she had developed an uncanny loathing for my dad and because she and I were also at loggerheads much of the time she seemed to lump us together and think of us as the enemy. She had no problem with my brother because he was still little and so just obeyed her. I remember lying in bed at night and trying to get to sleep as mum and dad argued in their room next door to mine. My mother's voice would rise and I'd hear foul language and I would hear dad's voice, quiet and strained.

I began to think a lot about suicide. I would lie in bed listening to my parents arguing and fantasise about what it would be like to slash my wrists and then go into their room and drip blood all over them while they lay in bed. I wanted an outlet for the intense distress I was feeling. When I no longer felt able to cope I went into town, bought myself a knife and slashed my wrists in a park near my friend's house. Afterwards I went and rang on her doorbell and waited for someone to answer the door, tears streaming down my face, my arms hanging down by my sides and blood dripping all over the doorstep. Being a practical person, her mother brought me inside and calmly held my wrists under cold water, bandaged them and then, after ringing my father she bundled me off to the casualty department at the local hospital where my father was anxiously waiting. I hadn't managed to sever any arteries but I had to have stitches and be assessed by the psychiatrist on duty. Having satisfied himself that the incident was a 'cry for help' I was allowed to go. I remember afterwards feeling relieved that dad now knew how much I was struggling and that I needed him to look out for me even though he was already coping with so much. When I got home mum just looked at me scornfully and told me I was stupid.

Things reached an unacceptable level when the situation began to manifest itself outside of the home even to the point of my mother writing letters to my father's bosses telling them that he was demon-possessed.

My father thought maybe a holiday away from us all would help my mother, so he sent her off to Morocco for a week feeling that the African sunshine would do her good but she, apparently, made an awful scene out there when it was time to return home and when she got back her behaviour was worse than ever.

One day there was a knock on the door and two men from the Criminal Investigation Department stood on our doorstep. Apparently my mother had rung and reported that father was having an incestuous relationship with me. After my father and I had answered some mortifying questions it soon became apparent, from mum's ranting throughout the interview, where the true problem lay. Later on, the police psychiatrist advised dad to submit his divorce papers as soon as possible. Even still, my brother had to be removed from the home (some friends of ours offered to look after him for a while), but we were allowed to bring him home after a few days.

Shortly after that my mother ran off with a man. From what I can gather she somehow persuaded him to take her away with him. In any event she made a public nuisance of herself and the next thing I remember she had been forcefully removed to the psychiatric wing of the local hospital where she was heavily sedated. After a few days it was revealed that she had suffered a mental break-down and she was diagnosed with hyper-mania, a mental disorder in which one suffers severe highs followed by severe lows. This certainly seemed to account for her extreme mood swings. I can't remember how long she was in hospital for but I didn't go to visit her. My father said that the scene was too disturbing and that it was heart-wrenching to see my mother amongst the other patients, wandering around like a zombie. My father said it was best that I didn't take her reverse charge calls from the hospital but it's hard to describe just how I felt when I was asked by the operator if I would and I had to refuse.

I was at college taking my 'A' levels by this time; I was nineteen and my brother was eight. My friend had gone to the States on a year's student exchange programme and I was feeling very much alone although I still spent most of my free time at her house (I'd been given a door key) mostly during the day while the family were out – I would take their dog for long walks in the park. Everything in life seemed irrelevant, trivial and of little consequence compared to what was happening to my family. I went through the motions of going to college each day but was not really getting anywhere with my studies. The future looked bleak. I knew that I wanted a chance to see how things would work out between myself and my boyfriend as I didn't feel that I could move on or have other relationships with the opposite sex until I'd done so. He was now twenty three, he'd left the police force and had moved down to Johannesburg, in South Africa and, having decided that he didn't want to join the South African police force, he had found work in a furniture company as a credit controller. After writing to him telling him of my thoughts he arranged my flight and bought my air ticket.

When the time came for me to leave I was more than ready to go. I had sat my 'A' level exams (later finding out that I had failed them, as I'd expected) and my mother had been home from hospital once or twice to see how she would settle back into home life. She was still in a zombie-like state and sometimes she would stand on the spot and rock from one foot to the other which I found utterly disturbing. This will sound callous but I felt no sympathy for her and, because I felt that she was shamming, I would get impatient with her. I didn't want to be there when she got home, and I certainly didn't want to be sitting in the house with her day in and day out, on the dole, while I tried to figure out what I was going to do with my life.

My father and brother took me to Heathrow Airport and there I waved goodbye to my little brother whom I wasn't going to see again for another eight years. And there began the next phase of my journey.

⚜

Chapter Two

"Go out into the darkness and put your hand into the hand of God..."

Unexpected tears of joy streamed down my face, the soft pink light of an African sunrise slowly filling the aircraft, as I took in the panorama below me. Plains stretched out before me as far as the eye could see. In all directions there appeared to be no beginning and no end – in sharp contrast to tiny England, whose southern coastline was almost completely visible from the aircraft as we departed. A thin ribbon of road split the landscape and ran almost as straight as an arrow past the odd circular reservoir dotted here and there in the distance.

As I stepped onto the runway at Jan Smuts airport, blinking in the sunlight, the smell of warm tarmac, dry grass and dust filling my nostrils, I was filled with an overwhelming sense of being at home. In no time at all I was through customs, had collected my luggage and was trotting through the airport with my trolley, dressed in my 1980s denim skirt and legwarmers. As I moved through the arrivals area a short, stocky man, who looked vaguely familiar, appeared to be smiling and waving at me and after a few seconds I came to the shocked realisation that it was my boyfriend. The last time I'd seen him, five years earlier, he'd been a youth in police uniform. The man before me now was bearded and dressed in office attire. We greeted each other shyly and made our way to his vehicle and as we spun along the city highways towards central Johannesburg I gazed out the window at the mine dumps and office blocks as they slid past. After unpacking and settling in we went out to dinner and to the drive-in with his cousin, who was studying at University and whom I'd met once or twice in Rhodesia, and a group of their friends. They greeted me warmly and after a short while it became clear that I had been much discussed and that I was welcome there. From day one we felt like a couple. We seemed to be viewed as such by his friends and without conscious thought I slipped into the little niche that seemed to have been created for me. Once he had shaved off his beard (it had to go!) and I'd seen him dressed in casual wear he looked younger and more like himself and we grew more comfortable together. While he was out at work that first week I cleaned out the flat, shopped for groceries at the supermarket across the road and cooked. He lived like a typical bachelor and didn't look after himself properly, existing on a very poor diet. I could clean, iron and prepare simple meals.

By the end of the first week I was already feeling so at home that I wanted to stay permanently in South Africa. He was enthusiastic about the idea so I wrote home telling family of my decision. Only much later, when I saw how my own two children get on and especially how they were a comfort for each other through all our difficult times, did I think about how my brother must have felt when he realised that his big sis wasn't coming home and even now when I think about it I feel a stab of pain because, from what I can understand, he went through a rough time after I left.

We encountered problems at the immigration office. After we had explained our situation and that I wished to remain in the country indefinitely they told us that as I was a dependent and not able to support myself I must return to England after my holiday period was up. We hadn't expected this as we just assumed that if my husband was willing to support me we'd be fine. Thinking on our feet we told them we were thinking of getting married, to which they replied that if we produced a marriage certificate within 6 months I would be allowed to stay. We did not face this thought with trepidation, it just seemed the natural thing to do as if it were just matter of course. So on 2nd December 1983 we were married, I was nineteen years old and just six months out of college. It was a court wedding, a small but happy affair, I wore a borrowed wedding dress which fitted me perfectly and flowers in my hair. My husband's family, who had come down from Zimbabwe, arranged a reception at the house where my sister-in-law was living at the time. My parents sent us a cheque, so that we could choose a wedding gift for ourselves, and wished us all the best. I can only imagine what my father must have thought about all this but there was nothing he could do from such a distance, apart from hope for the best.

In the meantime I had begun working, my first job, as an office junior at the head office of a large corporation. A person we knew, who was friends with someone in the personnel department, had put in a word for me and arranged an interview. All they were looking for, they said, was someone who was willing to work hard and be flexible. When I started, the year end audit was being carried out so I began by doing lots of photocopying for the auditors as well as handling the petty cash and doing switchboard relief. I'm sure we could have re-evaluated our position as far as immigration was concerned, now I was at least able to help support myself financially, but we went ahead with the wedding anyway – I don't think we even thought twice about it.

After just a couple of months cracks started to appear in our relationship. We were both young, immature, hot-headed and emotionally hurt. Differences in opinion degenerated into huge arguments. My teenage years in England had changed me considerably and although still very demure, I had managed to pick up some choice expletives. While I'd been chatting and laughing with my husband and his friends, on the day I arrived, I told a coarse joke which I thought was fairly mild. Everyone went into fits of giggles. I think the thing was that I looked so quiet and girlish that it was the last thing anyone expected to hear coming out of my mouth. But the look of disapproval from my husband to be was unmistakable and to add to it although I enjoyed a range of music, it now included rock, which he didn't like.

By the same token I noticed how, when we went out, the guys would invariably drink themselves into a drunken stupor whereas for us girls to do so would have been frowned upon. The age-old double standard. Right from the beginning I couldn't tolerate seeing him drunk. The outcome was that I lost all respect for him.

Being young and naïve I thought that our problems would, in time, iron themselves out. The trouble was that because they went unresolved they escalated instead and with each violent disagreement, with accusations being flung to and fro, we hurt each other and damaged our relationship increasingly. This was so far removed from what I'd envisaged for myself. I'd wanted acceptance, friendship, companionship and romance in my marriage. I felt that if things went well under my own roof I would find the stability and security needed to cope with everything outside of the home. I was quaint in my way of thinking and all I wanted was to be a good wife and mother. I even used to read church literature about it which had given me very constructive goals as far as marriage and motherhood went. For me divorce was not an option, I abhorred it, even though I was to use it as a threat during arguments in the years to come. I was very fond of his family and his friends. They had all become part of my life and I didn't want to hurt anyone. At home with my parents I knew I could eventually leave and put all the unhappiness behind me, but in my mind this was forever. This was when depression really began to take root.

I thought about what we should do. It seemed to me that if we were ever going to get anywhere we needed some guidance, at least a set of rules or principles that we could live by because it was obvious that we had no proper answers to our problems within ourselves. So one day I asked him how he would feel about going back to church. My family had stopped attending when my mother began to get ill and he had stopped when he joined the police. He was so pleased at the idea, he said he'd thought about it and often wanted to go back. When we told his parents they were overjoyed.

Our church was once an old covenant church. Over the years the church's understanding of the new covenant has grown and it is no longer a focal point what day or days we worship on, but at the time we met on Saturdays. To enable us to go my husband decided to change his job because Saturday was his company's busiest trading day and he had to work. Taking a leap of faith he resigned from his job immediately, before he had secured employment elsewhere, and we began attending church.

In my husband's line of work we soon found that those companies with vacancies were looking for people who could work Saturdays and in the end he had to resort to trying his hand at different things. This resulted in him going through a whole string of jobs that didn't come to anything, sales jobs where the earnings were commission only and companies that went under soon after he was taken on. Although I had worked my way up a little in the company (having taken over from someone who had left, a position with more responsibility) and had been given a good increase I wasn't earning enough to support us and pay all the bills. On my grocery budget all I could afford was the essentials – bread, milk, eggs, cheese, butter and basic toiletries. Luckily for me at least the company provided its staff with a hot lunch daily. Very often the caterer would let me take the leftovers home for my husband. The company was very good to me, when I got married they held a Kitchen Tea for me and the generous gifts I received pretty well equipped our kitchen; when I turned twenty one they threw a little surprise birthday party for me and a year later when I became pregnant with my son they threw a baby shower for me where, again, the gifts were so generous I had just about all I needed for my first child and to add to this my mother-in-law (his family were now also living in Johannesburg) threw a baby shower for me and I received an unbelievable amount of gifts from all the family and friends who supported it.

By the time our son was born in 1986, my husband had at last managed to find himself a good and steady job. It paid the bills and he was fairly happy there. I stopped working and with the pension money that I was paid out we furnished our bachelor flat (we were now living in a suburb just on the outskirts of the city) and made it comfortable to live in, replacing the old bits of furniture that we'd had till then.

We couldn't afford to buy our own home so we rented. We were always blessed with a roof over our heads. When our son was ten months old we moved to a two bedroomed cottage which became available when friends of ours, who had been renting the property, decided to move on. It was a similar situation in 1989, the year that our daughter was born, when we were looking for a three bedroomed property away from the city and close to my in laws. A couple in the church were looking to vacate a large property where the rent was reasonable, so we took the house over from them and my husband started commuting by train into the city, the train station being five minutes' walk from our house.

I loved the house, it was light and airy and spacious and all the bedrooms faced onto the lovely back yard.

By now we had been married six years and had sought much help in sorting out our differences, counselling with one minister after another, and telling our story over and over again. We had both been baptised and we had listened to countless sermons on how to have a happy marriage. We acknowledged the value of prayer and bible study but we couldn't find answers to our specific problems. Perhaps we weren't able to clearly define our difficulties. We should really have gone for marriage guidance counselling but we always assumed that we wouldn't be told anything that could not be found between the covers of the Bible. What we lacked was practical advice on such subjects as communication, trust, finances and how to raise our children. Although my husband's drinking had ceased when we went back to church, and with sister-in-law and my mother-in-law's good influences I had changed and become more refined in my manner as I tried to gain my husband's approval, the children had been born into an environment of conflict, unresolved problems and financial difficulties that had really taken a toll on our marriage. I was easily emotionally manipulated by my husband, but on the other hand I was manipulative myself, and this led to a breakdown of trust in our relationship just as it had occurred in my relationship with my mother.

I struggled to cope with daily living and I had no energy to be able to cope with the children even though they were the easiest of children to look after. I always made sure they were nicely dressed because I never wanted them to feel different to other children so that they became self-conscious and I'd wanted to be able to take them on outings to fun places but there was never any spare cash for this. I had finally got my driver's licence in 1989 when I was six months pregnant with our daughter but while I was in the maternity home with her our car was stolen and we couldn't replace it as we had never been able to afford insurance. This meant that I was housebound, apart from going out for walks around the neighbourhood, alone in the house day after day with two little children to keep occupied. I was dependent on people to be able to get out and do things like grocery shopping. I couldn't spend time with my sister-in-law or my mother-in-law without feeling that I was imposing on them and I disliked feeling like a nuisance. I also struggled with feelings of jealousy towards my sister-in-law. Observing the strong mother-daughter relationship between them left me feeling excluded. This was completely unfounded as my mother-in-law is the sort of person who is incapable showing any sort of favouritism. The problem stemmed from me.

A deep sense of loneliness set in, and not just because I spent so much time alone. my husband and I both knew, deep down, that we truly cared about one another and yet we tended to bring out the worst in each other. On the other hand, *because* we cared about one another we, at times, also brought out the best in each other. I think my parents' relationship showed me how complicated love can be. My father's love for my mother taught me what true love is and just how much it can endure.

I dreaded my husband going to work in the mornings leaving me to face another day on my own and yet when he was at home we more often than not would get into an argument. I remember how I would pray every morning that we wouldn't fight that evening, and then when we did fight, day after day, I began to feel like such a hypocrite. As he was just about the only person I was seeing in a day, and I was measuring my feelings of self-worth against our relationship alone, I began to detest myself. With all the bickering I felt hateful and my husband's reactions to me and my behaviour were negative, compounding my feelings of self-loathing. I was very conscious of the fact that my depression was very hard on the children and if I could have snapped out of it I would have, but I felt completely helpless to be able to do anything about it. I dreaded the fact that I might also be mentally ill and was terrified that what happened to my mother was going to happen to me. In so many arguments I'd been told that I was just like her.

In my misery I was like a wounded animal, and with the slightest provocation I would turn on my family, snapping and snarling. I questioned the fickleness of human love. It just made no sense. I'm not sure that I can adequately convey the self-hatred and self-loathing that I was contending with.

In 1991 dad brought me over to England for a couple of months for a holiday. He had come out to visit in 1990, when our daughter was a few weeks old, and it had been the first time I saw him since I'd left home. By then he and my mother had divorced and my mother was remarried. After the divorce my father and brother began to see more of the family in England and my brother got to know his cousins and feel more like a family member. When we came over in 1991 my brother was sixteen years old. Although he spent most of his time out with his friends we got on very well and he really enjoyed having the children around. Over that time I spent a lot of time with my old schoolfriend, who was now married herself but as yet had no children, and she enjoyed the kids too, helping me out with taking care of them.

My husband came over and joined us for the last month of our visit, his first trip overseas. A few months previously he had got a new job working for his best friend from his police days in Zimbabwe. We had been promised better pay and the opportunity to train, as he had been keen for some time on the idea of doing a book-keeping course. The pay was good but the offer of training didn't materialise, and then the friend's business partner talked him into getting rid of my husband, which he did over the phone while we were still in the UK.

When we got back to South Africa my husband had no job, plus we had spent money while we had been on holiday including, of course, his air fare and we were already in much credit card debt. With the political change that was taking place in South Africa, where affirmative action was being enforced, and changes in the work place in general especially in my husband's line of work which was credit control, he was now unable to find work.

Once again we found ourselves in the position where we had no money to buy food. I was back to buying just the essentials again, and this time we couldn't even pay our rent. I tried to look for work, myself, but had been out of the work place for so long that my skills were rusty and there were so many applicants for each job that I didn't stand a chance. We claimed what unemployment benefits we were entitled to but that didn't last us long. Church friends kindly helped us out with groceries when they could but apart from that we were down to eating porridge and scrambled eggs for dinner on alternate nights and I was tearful at times as I put the children's meagre dinners down before them and they dutifully ate them never once complaining. Our son was six years old by then and should have been starting at school but we couldn't afford the school fees.

With the increasing political unrest in South Africa security was also becoming a problem. Our house had a large garden with an enclosed courtyard and, although I loved the house, I began to feel extremely vulnerable there as it was easy to gain access to the property and anyone could walk around the back of the house and through the courtyard to the back door. On a couple of occasions there was a knock on the back door and an African would be standing on the doorstep asking for water to drink. I also felt extremely vulnerable whenever my husband was away as we had large windows with no burglar bars on them and no security gates on the doors, those being the norm in other homes. Our landlord didn't have any fitted and because the house was not our own we didn't want to incur the expense of having them fitted ourselves. I would lie at night plotting how, if someone broke in, I would escape from the house unharmed with both children, as burglars more often than not attacked anyone in their path. We had already been burgled once, just before our daughter was born.

Over all this time I was in regular contact with my father, who was very concerned for us, and who, at the end of 1992, suggested that the best thing for us all would be to return to England. At first I balked at the idea as I felt I could never be happy in England, but dad reassured me that once I was living there and settled in my own home I'd be fine. With a heavy heart I began to pack up the house and sell things. The whole ordeal was extremely stressful and once the flights had been booked there was a time constraint. And as I worked at packing and sorting day by day I began to feel very ill.

After bidding painful farewells to family and friends, the children and I left first at the end of February 1993. After selling the rest of the furniture and tying up loose ends, such as paying off our debt, my husband followed a month later.

❄

Chapter Three

"That shall be to you better than light and safer than a known way…"

We arrived in England, just as my family had fifteen years before, with just our suitcases. As always, though, we were blessed from the start with a roof over our heads. One of my dad's neighbours, who lived in one property in the row of houses where he lived, owned another three bedroomed property, which he rented out. Dad arranged with him that we would rent the property and he paid the deposit and first month's rent for us. Because I was alone with the children, as soon as I arrived, I was able to claim income support as I was classified as a single parent. The housing department took over our rent payments and we were refunded our first month's rent which I paid back to dad. The house was very pleasant and comfortable, fully furnished with a little garden which the owner liked to maintain. After making the necessary arrangements our son started at school and our daughter began attending the local playgroup.

Once in the school system, the children went through the routine procedure of having eyesight and hearing tests and it was discovered that our son had a lazy eye so he had to start wearing an eye patch, over the good eye, and glasses. As we couldn't afford to pay for glasses privately he wore big brown National Health ones and it changed his appearance. In addition to this, as we had arrived in the middle of an English winter, the children began to wear warm winter clothing including thick jackets. All of a sudden their appearance had changed drastically from the little children who would run around in shorts, T-shirts and sandals and I hardly recognised them anymore, which I found very painful. I felt very confused and disorientated, I would look for items, such as a pair of scissors, and had to think whether I had them; where I had put them or whether I had left them behind. I know now that this is very common when such an enormous move takes place, it is very disruptive in someone's life and I think especially as you get older. Also with the complete change of environment and routine I would forget little every day things that I used to do in South Africa, like how I used to sing songs to the children and read to them at bed time and how on Saturday mornings, when I had a lie in, I would put out a plate of biscuits for them and their container of Lego so that they had something to munch on and something to keep them occupied until I got up. Even now I suddenly remember some possession that we used to have or a favourite recipe that I'd forgotten ever making.

When my husband arrived our family was reclassified in the social system. I now received unemployment benefits and had to report to the job centre where I was told that, although he was not permitted to seek employment as he did not have the necessary visa, I had to look for work as he could look after the children. I had to report periodically what progress I was making in finding employment and if I was having difficulty there was a variety of free government training courses available to me. After a few months I went to college and took a three month course in business administration updating my office skills. I really enjoyed the course and also enjoyed meeting new people.

After a lengthy process my husband received his permanent residence and set about looking for work. Early in 1994 he was taken on at British Telecom, in their finance department, starting in a temporary position which later became permanent. We were now financially independent but after paying the bills there was not much left over as our rent was high. The person who owned our property decided that he no longer wanted to rent it out. We couldn't understand why as we kept the house clean and tidy, whereas the people who had lived there before us had left the house in a real mess. We began looking for another home but found the rents very high in the area and because we had no furniture we either had to find another furnished house or we had to suddenly buy ourselves a house full of furniture as well as paying a high rent. We wanted to stay in the area because we didn't want the children to have to change schools – we wanted some stability for them as we felt they had been through enough upheaval. Dad suggested that we should stay put in the house where we were, just continue paying the rent, and see what the owner would do. Eventually he began eviction proceedings which gave us the authority to sign up on the housing list at the housing department. Because we were a family with young children we were on the priority housing list and as soon as our eviction date was set, early in 1995, we were offered a house on the other side of town to where we were living. As far as housing was concerned this house turned out to be our biggest blessing of all to date, although at the time it was one of a row of very drab looking houses in what was considered to be a not-so-good neighbourhood. As it was a council property the rent was exceedingly low and, because we didn't mind second-hand goods apart from beds and electrical appliances, we decided to take out a short term loan which paid for all our furniture as well as our first holiday back to South Africa (since that holiday we have been back every three years so that the children could be with the family and so that the family didn't miss out too much on the children as they were growing up). Another huge blessing concerned the children's schooling. Our biggest concern about moving was having to move them to another school and for a while this really upset me. I had unsuccessfully appealed to the housing department explaining our family's situation in moving from South Africa. After we moved I continued taking the children to their school on two buses. Each day, by the time I had taken the two buses home again, it was just about time to set out and pick them up as they finished school mid- afternoon. One day we were at a barbeque with some church friends (as we continued attending church services) and I was busy chatting to a lady who happened to be a school teacher, and explaining our situation to her, when she invited me to go and take a look at the school where she taught. A few days later I got on the bus to this school, with the children. The bus headed away from town, into the countryside to a nearby village where we hopped off and walked the rest of the way. We walked along a tiny little footpath and there we came across this little building nestled amongst tall leafy trees and surrounded on two sides by the fields of the neighbouring farm. Inside, the classrooms were spacious, clean and comfortable and as it happened the lady whom I'd spoken to became my daughter's first teacher at the school and today she is one of my dearest friends. As I rode home on the bus with the children my heart was filled with elation and praise for how God works in our lives.

We bought my brother's little car, as he was upgrading his vehicle, and in 1995 I got my British driver's licence after taking my test again (South African licences were not valid for use in England at the time) so I could now take the children to school instead of them getting lifts or going on the bus. I used to help out at the school listening to children read and clearing up paint pots in the art area. I started my first job in 1997, when my school teacher friend told me of a friend of hers who lived on a farm and was looking for a reliable lady to clean her large farmhouse twice a week. As well as this I got a job working at the local playgroup. I didn't earn a lot but put my earnings to good use and felt glad that I could now buy a few things for the children. I remember, when after saving up I had bought my son a bicycle, the look on his face, when he woke up to find a gleaming new bicycle at the bottom of his bed, was absolutely priceless. After cleaning for about a year, I went to an employment agency to look for work. This agency recruited catering and office staff so I went and enquired about catering. During the interview I was asked whether I'd ever done office work so I explained that I'd worked for a while but had taken time off to raise a family, although I'd recently done an administration course. So I started, first of all, with a three week assignment doing filing, part time, for an insurance company. This gave me the boost of confidence that I needed because it was so straightforward. After that I was given a three month assignment working at a small budget airline in their revenue accounts department. My earnings were very reasonable and I went through a period of buying whatever clothes I wanted, a very new experience for me. This freedom enabled me to get over my complex, which I'd carried from childhood, about my appearance, and it gave me immense satisfaction and enjoyment to provide for my children.

The great thing about working at the airline was that staff could fly, paying just airport taxes. We all went to Italy spending a few days in Rome, where we also stayed in discounted accommodation. I also took the children, by myself - on a trip which I financed - to Spain, where we spent a week in Barcelona. At first I was terrified as I had never taken the children away, on my own, to a foreign country, where I didn't speak the language.

I had taken Spanish at college but it was very elementary, I was amazed though at what I remembered and actually managed to get around quite capably, as well as cope with using the currency, which was pesetas at the time. We stayed in bed and breakfast accommodation in the residential part of the city, where English was not spoken as much as in the touristy part of the city, down by the seafront. We found a little restaurant which we ended up eating at every day, where I found that, with a little help from the staff there, who were very friendly and got to know us, I could order meals for the three of us without too much effort. We spent the holiday doing all the sorts of things the children could enjoy, we got on the train and went to a nearby seaside resort where we swam and played on the beach and we visited places like the aquarium and the Imax 3-D cinema. It was an experience that gave me a shot of confidence.

One aspect of being at work was that it helped me to gain a little independence, especially financial. Because I was terribly nervous it took a lot of courage but I was meeting and interacting with people and I found the work interesting and stimulating as I had always been interested in travel. I was still struggling at home but didn't take my personal problems to work and I never got to know anyone well enough to actually confide in them. I would never invite anyone to our house because I felt that it was not a happy place to invite people to, and we had so often had a fight just as we were about to go out and visit friends or have friends over to have a meal with us and, most of all, it was at home that I struggled with my depression the most. Domestic unhappiness is terribly destructive in the sense that it is like living with an 'enemy within' and can erode one's ability to function outside of the home.

We were a mixed crowd, university students would come and go as there was much temporary work available during the holidays and there were also a lot of foreign speaking staff – French, German, Spanish and Italian – representing the destinations that we flew to. There was a good atmosphere about the place, lively, and much of the time there was a great carry on with much banter and laughter. Sadly, though, in the accounts department rumours began to go around that the company was floundering financially and finally, late in 1999, we got to work one day and were all told to go home as the company had gone into administration.

Just before the company went under I had started taking Prozac, an antidepressant drug, to enable me to cope with my nerves a little better, but I started having panic attacks (which is a common side-effect) and came off it immediately. The panic attacks carried on for a few months and I found them very disturbing and frightening. They would often strike at night time and I would lie awake all night fighting them off. Also, I had stopped going to church some time before. I had reached the point where I felt like I was such a hypocrite, I could no longer go along to church and pretend that we were a happy family. People at church asked after me frequently but my absence was nothing unusual as there were often days when I couldn't even bring myself to get out of bed, let alone go to church, so it was a common occurrence. (I never called into work sick because I didn't want to leave them short-staffed). Another factor was that, as I was quiet and never committed myself to getting involved in church activities or service, as I've mentioned previously, I gave the impression that I kept myself to myself and was, therefore, not easily approachable. This was confirmed to me some time later, when a someone, who is now another of my closest friends, told me that she'd seen me at church over the years and had wanted to make friends with me, but got the impression that I was very much a private person. My shyness and quietness had always been a problem for me and I was aware that it was easy for people to view it as unfriendliness. I found it difficult to make friends, to feel comfortable with people, and felt that when I spoke I came across awkwardly – I never had found it easy to make small talk. I also felt that the more people got to know me the less they had reason to like me. This was exacerbated by the fact that, because I had a South African accent, I felt like I was a foreigner and that I didn't fit in.

I also stopped praying. I remember how, after not praying for a long while, I tried to do so as I drove to work one day. I started saying a few words but I just couldn't bring myself to carry on, I was saying the same old words that I always used to say, "Please God, help us not to fight tonight," and I just couldn't bring myself to do it, I felt too much of a hypocrite and too guilty to pray. I had always acknowledged and needed God in my life but I thought, surely, He could not want to listen to me anymore.

I was now out of work so no longer bringing in an income. I was sitting alone at home feeling trapped in our negative home environment day after day, and I was still struggling with the panic attacks. Physically, mentally and emotionally I was in a state, and in fear of having a breakdown at any moment. Thoughts clamoured in my head day and night until one day I put on my coat and headed into town, to the Citizens Advice Bureau.

Chapter Four

"So I went forth and finding the hand of God, trod gladly into the night…"

"Divorce is a tough business and you have to be strong to be able to get through it. You are not strong, I don't think you could handle it."

Over the past few years, since we'd arrived in England, I had often resorted to visiting the Citizens Advice Bureau to obtain information to guide us through whatever process we were going through at the time, changing from income support to unemployment benefits, applying for permanent residence, our rights versus the landlord's concerning the house that we'd rented and how to negotiate the process we needed to go through with the Housing Department to obtain a council property.

It was just after New Year – the new Millenium, and the young chap sat before me, his eyes full of concern, as I asked him how one goes about initiating divorce proceedings. Before giving me an answer, he probed a little into my background and, because his manner was so friendly and approachable, and because I had not talked – really talked – to anyone for so long, somehow it all came pouring out in a torrent. I told him about my feelings concerning my mum, and about my loneliness. (Feelings which were often intertwined when, for instance, I'd take the children swimming at the public pool and would ache as I watched mothers and grandmothers splashing around with their charges). I also told him my feelings about God, about my marriage and the children, our life in South Africa and about my depression and my fear of what might happen to me – that I might end up like my mother. I was on drugs to help me to sleep at night and to calm me and I was clearly groggy from them and generally in bad shape. After listening to me in thoughtful silence, he gave me one of the best pieces of advice I've ever received. "Mrs Robas," he said, "you need to talk to someone. These are major issues and they need sorting out. You need to talk to a friend, a priest, a doctor, a psychiatrist and a marriage guidance counsellor."

I left his office feeling lighter and with the first glimmer of hope that I'd felt in a long time. Looking back, I honestly feel that God – after observing my floundering for so long - had grabbed me by the scruff of my neck and pulled me back from the edge. I was finally in a state where He could reach me and begin working with me.

As is possible with a malleable piece of clay, and like the pot mentioned in Jeremiah 18, although I had become mis-shaped, I could be remoulded and formed into a new vessel.

> But the pot he was shaping from the clay
> was marred in his hands; so the potter
> formed it into another pot, shaping it
> as seemed best to him.
>
> *Jeremiah 18:4*

Chapter Five

"And He led me towards the hills and the breaking of day in the lone east."

"Jehovah never, *ever* turns His back on us," my next door neighbour said turning in her Bible to Hebrews 13: 5. This was in answer to a question whose answer was critical to the elimination of my feelings of utter isolation and loneliness: "Can we ever bring about a situation where God refuses to listen to our prayers, to hear us when we call out to Him for help?" I had told her how I had stopped praying because I felt like such a hypocrite, the result being that I felt cut off from my only real source of help and comfort. She then went on to explain that no sin on earth is too great not to be covered by Christ's sacrifice, and that when He died He made it possible for us to be in God's presence for ever – 2 Corinthians 5:18 & 19 "All this is from God, Who reconciled us to Himself through Christ and gave us the ministry of reconciliation: that God was reconciling the world to Himself in Christ, not counting men's sins against them," continuing in verse 21, "God made Him Who had no sin to be sin for us, so that in Him we might become the righteousness of God" and Col 1:19 – 22 "For God was pleased to have all His fullness dwell in him, and through Him to reconcile to Himself all things, whether things on earth or things in heaven, by making peace through His blood, shed on the

45

cross. Once you were alienated from God and were enemies in your minds because of your evil behaviour. But now He has reconciled you by Christ's physical body through death to present you holy in His sight, without blemish and free from accusation."

My neighbour is a Jehovah's Witness and a very kind, caring and approachable individual. When I walked out of the Citizens Advice Bureau that day she was the first person I turned to for help; help in getting me back on track and restoring to me something too valuable to put a price tag on, my relationship with God.

It so happened that the Witnesses had begun a series on the life of Christ, as their study topic, just as I started going along to their Bible studies. I don't believe that this is coincidental, just as I don't believe that it was by coincidence that I happened to speak to that particular advisor at the Citizens Advice Bureau that day.

I believe that once I had arrived at the point where God could actually reach me, He then took me by the hand and led me to all those places where I needed to be, in order to hear what He wanted me to hear.

At the Bible studies I learned all about Jesus and His family and His life on earth, and by the time we had completed the series Jesus was real to me and no longer some long, haired ethereal being who floated two inches above the ground. I learned that He came to live on earth in human form to live like you and me so that He could understand us, our lives, our difficulties and our temptations and He came to die for us so that He could save us from eternal death as explained in Hebrews 2:14 – 18, "Since the children (you and I) have flesh and blood, He too shared in their humanity so that by His death He might destroy him who holds the power of death – that is, the devil – and free those who all their lives were held in slavery by their fear of death. For surely it is not the angels He helps but Abraham's descendants (you and

I). For this reason He had to be made like His brothers in every way, in order that He might become a merciful and faithful high priest in the service of God, and that He might make atonement for the sins of the people. Because He Himself suffered when He was tempted, He is able to help those who are being tempted."

I had been going to church for years, had started at an early age, but contrary to what you might expect, my Bible knowledge was very limited and because I had never read the Bible right the way through from beginning to end, it was extremely disjointed. As one of our church pastors recently said to me there is a big difference between being associated with a church for years and actively being part of one. I had always been taught about God, but now I also had a very sound understanding of Christ, and of the relationship between the Father and the Son.

I went to my neighbour's church a few times and got to know several members of the congregation, they were all very warm and friendly and I really enjoyed the talks and studies. After spending time with my neighbour and her family and getting to know them I have a deep regard and respect for them all, they are a lovely family and all the children have followed their parents in the faith. I have a lot of time and respect for Jehovah's Witnesses in general as they are extremely hard working and dedicated.

Eventually though, after my husband and I had been going to marriage guidance counselling for a while, I started going to our own church again as it was important to us to worship united as a family. This time I approached church with a confidence that was steadily growing all the time, my relationship with God intact, and a whole different attitude. I wanted to be accepted as a member of the congregation so set out right from the beginning to attend services regularly and consistently as I knew that this is what I needed to do to prove myself to the people there and to gain credibility. After a while I began to feel confident that I was viewed as someone who was committed and no longer as someone who came and went. I took another step forward and signed up for tea duty once a month, the first time I had ever committed myself to a regular responsibility. With my new confidence I was succeeding in being far more outgoing and began getting to know people at church a lot better and forming friendships. As I conversed with others we, naturally, talked at times about problems and difficulties and as I listened I began to realise that I had much in common with other people and that I had experienced a lot of what they had been or were going through. I could empathise with them and they with me and we were able to encourage each other. I found these conversations so uplifting, and realised that this is why we need to come together regularly in fellowship with one another – people need each other. On one occasion I was talking to a friend of mine who is also one of the song leaders and I mentioned that my daughter played the guitar and that quite often, at home, she would play and I would sing. I even went so far as to say that I would be happy for us to perform a song at church if the occasion ever arose. My friend held me to my word and one Saturday I sang my first song, a duet with another friend. I was so nervous about getting up in front of everyone and I shook the whole way through but I really enjoyed it. After that I began to get more and more involved with singing and worship. At first, I was so nervous that we had to set up and sing positioned on one side of the hall to the side of the congregation but eventually I grew in confidence and we were able to move to the front of the church facing the congregation. Previously we had mostly used CD's for our worship music but now a couple of people had begun bringing musical instruments and my daughter would play her guitar and we ended up performing live music which the congregation really seemed to enjoy. From that time on I went from strength to strength. On one occasion we were short of song leaders so I was asked if I would fill in. My attitude was 'give it a go', so I did, and began to regularly lead the congregation in worship.

On another occasion we were short of speakers for our Ladies' Day and I was asked if I would give a talk, so again I said I would 'give it a go'. I prepared and gave a book review on 'The Power of a Praying Wife' by Stormie Omartian and once I led the worship. Every time I was approached to help or do something new I accepted enthusiastically knowing that with God's help, which I always immediately prayed for, I would succeed. The key to it all was that I was growing in God-confidence, not self-confidence and this was giving me the courage to step completely out of my comfort zone and take on things that, previously, I would have been too afraid to try. Now I find that I get so much more out of the services because I am actively involved and participating instead of observing. I seem to absorb so much more and have become so enthused and energetic. It's true what people say, "what you put into something is what you get out of it."

I would recommend marriage guidance counselling to any couple who are committed to each other but who are experiencing difficulties in their relationship. We had the same counsellor each week and it was so beneficial to have a third person present at our discussions who was unbiased and impartial. Over a period of time we described and brought out into the open the whole of our married life together and methodically addressed and dealt with all of the different problem areas and issues one by one. With each problem that was brought up we described how we had handled (or rather mis-handled) it and our counsellor would say "Do you see, Julie, how it hurt my husband when you did this?" and "Do you see, my husband, how it hurt Julie when you did that?" The counsellor clearly defined and isolated our problems for us so that we could see clearly what we were dealing with and once she had done this they no longer seemed insurmountable. Somehow, sitting down and talking things over constructively produced, in itself, a healing effect. We felt that we were getting things out of our system but they were being filtered in a controlled environment, not one of anger and hostility.

We reached a point where we needed to bring into our discussions our Christian values so we continued our counselling sessions but this time with our pastor. The value of marriage guidance counselling training had, somewhere along the line, been recognised by our church and had been made available to the ministry so this time the approach in dealing with us was different. Thanks to our marriage guidance counsellor my husband and I were able to give a clear description of our challenges to our pastor who then proceeded to give us clear and precise guidelines as to how to tackle them.

In accordance with our pastor's advice we took control of our expenditure and with careful management of our finances we eventually paid off all our debt. The feeling of being debt free was absolutely amazing and I would never want to be bound by those chains again. We also bought our council house at a very discounted price (our first home of our own) and we saved up and purchased for me a new car of my own.

From the time my husband and I had got together I had wanted his acceptance and approval and had tried hard to change and improve myself in order to obtain it, even to the extent of curtailing my hobbies. This had run parallel to my Christian calling to change and become more God-like. Eventually, though, I began to question whether I was striving to become what God wanted me to be or what my husband wanted me to be. After thinking this over I sat down with him and explained that music and reading are important to me and part of who I am as a person.

I once again devoured books and over a period of time came across inspirational biographies, passages, poems and sayings which brought me much encouragement, many of which I have included in my anthology 'I Waited Patiently'.

Whatever life throws at me, deep down in my soul is a little light which burns steadily. It is a joy which has nothing to do with how I'm feeling, how I'm being treated, what is said to me or how my day is going, whether there exists fairness or unfairness but it is the assurance that I am His, He loves me with all my faults and flaws, I am forgiven all my past wrongs and each day that I arise in the morning I am a new creation and have a chance to begin again and move steadily forwards towards the destiny that God has for me, as His plan unfolds for all of us, along the way reaching out and helping as many people that I can, sharing the Good News of Hope and Joy everlasting in a world that desperately needs it and Him.

PART TWO

I Waited Patiently

An Anthology of Encouragement

Dedicated to

Gill Goode, Janie Gadsden, Becca Gentil and Sophie with love.

I waited patiently for the Lord;

He turned to me and heard my cry.

He lifted me out of the slimy pit,

out of the mud and mire;

He set my feet on a rock

and gave me a firm place to stand.

He put a new song in my mouth,

a hymn of praise to our God.

Psalm 40:1 - 3

Chapter Six

Jill

"Would you like to come on up, Julie?" Jill called down to me, where I was sitting waiting in reception, as she leaned over the stair rail, an armful of files and papers clutched to her chest. Her mop of wavy brown hair fell forward and framed her face as she peered down at me. We chatted easily as I followed her up the stairs and as we reached the office door she turned and asked me if I would reach into the front pocket of her slacks and pull out the key. As I did so I laughingly said to her, "I wouldn't do this to a bloke," and as she turned the key and leaned on the door holding onto the handle she rejoined, "No, not unless you knew him very well!" With that the door flew open and we fell into the office snickering and snorting. From that moment on we were firm friends.

Once I was back on my feet, early in 2000, I began working for Honeywell Network Solutions and was based at Vauxhall, the car manufacturers, in Luton. I worked there for two years until they decided to downsize their staff. What I really enjoyed about that period was the fact that one of my colleagues was South African and we got on well as we had a lot in common. The other thing was that two of the people there were Christians and for the first time I experienced how wonderful it is to work with fellow Christians. We all went to different churches but we had a common bond – I felt like we were singing from the same hymn sheet.

Shortly after I left Honeywell my school teacher friend told me about a friend of hers, Jill, who was working for a development company, a new business that was starting up in our area, and who was looking for part time help. I applied for and got the job starting there in April 2002.

I loved the job and I loved working with Jill. At first we occupied two rented offices in an office block, Jill and I shared one large office while our boss occupied a smaller one which could be reached through an adjoining door. The following year we moved to our own building and employed more staff. We were very blessed to each have our own work stations which were fitted out to our requirements. In our rented office, though, Jill and I sat at work stations opposite each other. We worked very comfortably and happily together - quietly much of the time, each absorbed with our own tasks, but we would break off occasionally to have a natter and a laugh. We both enjoyed reading and would often discuss what book we were reading at the time. Jill had a faith, although she didn't attend church, as she couldn't find one that she felt she could commit herself to and apart from this, she would often come into the office on a Sunday to catch up on filing and other jobs that tended to get neglected, due to the fact that her workload was so heavy. On Mondays I would tell her about what I had heard at church over the weekend and we would have great discussions about it and she would bring me interesting and inspirational books to read. I learned so much from those books. I think, as Christians, we can often feel that our purpose, when we come into contact with other people, is to teach them but I so often find that God puts people in my path so that I can learn from them (or else it is a two-way street). Ever since I had put my hand in God's, in total trust, I had felt that He was leading me into the path of different people for a reason and Jill was no exception. As well as being warm and funny (on one occasion she accidently came into the office with her trousers on inside out) she was exceedingly knowledgeable and could converse on many different topics. I found her incredibly interesting to listen to. She was also extremely hard working and competent at her job. From day one it was obvious that Jill had taken a liking to me and enjoyed my company, it showed in the way her face lit up when I walked into the office and she was forever hugging me. On the day that I was called into the boss's office and offered a permanent position at the company, we were no sooner out of the door than Jill threw her arms around me, her eyes full of tears and exclaimed, "I'm so *thrilled* that you've been made permanent!" When someone shows delight in your friendship like that it can make your spirits soar, and that was how she made me feel.

Jill was completely unpretentious and without guile, I trusted her completely – I knew she would never run me down behind my back and I trusted her with my feelings - and she exuded an absolute love of life. She so enjoyed her free time on the weekends, it didn't matter whether it was spent doing housework or going out or reading, and she loved her family.

In March 2004, just prior to my healing, she was diagnosed with lung cancer and was told that she had a matter of months, not years, to live. She was fifty four. Typically of her, she faced this bombshell in a matter of fact manner and carried on as usual, continuing at work as long as she could until she had to start carting her respirator around with her and it became impractical for her to continue any longer. We all tried to carry on as normal (we were now in our new offices and there were more of us) but it tore us all up to see Jill steadily lose weight and become increasingly short of breath. She had her good days and her bad days and sometimes she and I would be in the kitchen, for instance, making tea when she would say to me, "Julie, I need a hug," and I would put my arms around her and gently hold her for as long as she needed. We would stand there, two people locked in wordless grief, while the seemingly pointless hustle and bustle of business went on around us.

She developed pleurisy on several occasions and would have to go to the local hospice to have her lungs drained. On the last occasion her bedroom at home was furnished so that she could spend her remaining time comfortably. A hospital bed was brought in which could be adjusted so that she could sleep or lie in a raised position and she had a stand with all her tubes attached. Jill had expressed a wish to have her bedroom decorated, so while she was at the hospice and before all her equipment was installed, her husband Colin moved all the unnecessary bedroom furniture out of the room and then Gill and I painted the bedroom and washed, ironed and rehung the curtains. There developed, between Gill and myself, such bond that day as we worked together for the good of our dear mutual friend. When Colin tried to thank us for our efforts we told him that our motive was really quite selfish because it was something we *could* do, and it stopped us from feeling *so* helpless.

Jill's mum moved in with the family for the remaining months of Jill's life and took care of all of her personal needs with the help of the nurses who came in daily to check on her medication and to wash and dress her. The housework became a problem to cope with so when I asked him, my boss David, gave me permission to start work late every Thursday so that I could go and help with the heavy chores such as vacuuming the carpets and washing the kitchen floor – the sorts of jobs Jill's mum found difficult to handle. David, who was extremely fond of Jill, was only too glad to be able to help the family in some way and made it clear that he did not expect me to make up my hours. The good thing about working part time was that I could go and keep Jill company during the day, whereas most of her other friends could only visit after work hours. This also allowed her mother to have a break and to be able to go out for a while if she wanted or needed to, to go shopping or to the library.

One winter's day, before she became really ill, I wrapped Jill up warmly and took her out for a ride in my car as she was rarely able to get out of the house. We drove up onto the nearby downs and parked on the crest of a hill. It was so peaceful as she and I sat warm and snug in the car, Jill wrapped in a blanket, watching the world going on around us and people flying their kites in the cold winter wind – just two devoted friends enjoying every remaining moment together, one precious moment at a time.

On another occasion Jill was too ill to go out so she beckoned to me and patted a space on the bed beside her. As I climbed onto the bed and curled up next to her she slipped her arm through mine and we spent the afternoon listening to Christian music and where we could we sang along, praising God – she with her toes moving in time to the music. One evening my daughter came with me to visit Jill and brought her guitar along. She strummed and I sang a couple of songs, one of them being an absolute favourite of mine called 'Father of life, draw me closer'. This song was such a comfort to me through my depression and, because of the way it was worded; it is a song that I used to sing in the form of a prayer to God. I especially loved the part where it says, 'O Holy Spirit, saturate my soul, and let the life of God fill me now, let Your healing power breathe life and make me whole'. Every time I sang 'O Holy Spirit, saturate my soul' I would get a warm feeling in the whole of my chest which would comfort me, even if it was just for a little while – even just for the duration of the song. Eventually though, as in Psalm 40:1, God did hear my prayer, after I had waited patiently so many years for healing, God's Spirit *did* saturate my soul and His healing power *did* breathe life and made me whole – depression lost its grip on me and I became a whole person. Jill said to me afterwards that while I was singing she could feel that warmth of the Holy Spirit saturating *her* soul also, she was able to draw the same feeling of peace and comfort from the powerful words of that song that I once needed and experienced, just as I'd hoped she would.

As the days went by and her condition grew worse, Jill became weaker and weaker, but in spirit she remained strong right until the end. People have often said that when they went to visit her, to comfort and reassure her, it was *they* who came away reassured. Jill and I were able to speak frankly and openly about her pending death, I told her how much I cared about her and how much I was going to miss her but I said to her that we would always be best friends "no matter what." One day, just before the end, she told me that she believed that we could have been sisters.

She died peacefully in her sleep on the 14th November 2004. There was nothing ostentatious about her funeral, it was a simple affair, just as she had planned it before she died, but the church was packed with people. Her ashes now lie in an unmarked spot, in a beautiful little church yard in the village where she used to live and I drive past it and my eyes fleetingly rest on the spot every day, as I take Carly to college, and I thank God for His gift of our cherished friendship.

In my garden, right outside the patio doors where I can see it, there thrives a little rose bush with scented pink roses, which Jill turned up at the office with one day clutched in her arms – a little gift for me which she bought on a special offer for just £1. Words cannot express how grateful I am to God, that I was able to give back just a little of what Jill gave to me.

Father of life, draw me closer
(Let the peace of God reign)

Father of life, draw me closer,

Lord, my heart is set on You.

Let me run the race of time

With Your life enfolding mine,

And let the peace of God,

Let it reign.

O Holy Spirit, Lord, my comfort;

Strengthen me, hold my head up high.

And I stand upon Your truth,

Bringing glory unto You,

And let the peace of God,

Let it reign.

O Lord, I hunger for more of You;

Rise up within me,

Let me know Your truth.

O Holy Spirit, saturate my soul,

And let the life of God fill me now,

Let Your healing power breathe life and make me whole,

And let the peace of God,

Let it reign.

THE SHIP

I am standing on the sea shore. A ship at my side spreads her white sails to the morning breeze and starts for the blue ocean. She is on object of beauty and strength, and I stand and watch her till at length she is only a ribbon of white cloud just where the sea and sky come to mingle with each other.

Then someone at my side says, There she is gone! Gone? Gone where? Gone from my sight – that is all – she is just as long in mast and hull and spar as she was when she left my side, and just as able to bear her load of living freight to the place of destination. Her diminished size is in me – not in her, and just at the moment when someone at my side says, 'There! She is gone!' there are other voices ready to take up the glad shout, 'THERE! SHE COMES' –

and that is Dying.

Leonard Lyons

Just after Jill died a friend of mine lent me a copy of Fiona Castle's 'Rainbows Through the Rain' which she wrote after the death of her husband, Roy Castle – the popular TV entertainer, from cancer. In her book I found this beautiful poem, which I will always associate with Jill

Chapter Seven

Freda

"Allo Duck! 'Ow are ya?" Freda beamed at me as she leant on her walking frame in the doorway. I gave her a hug and a kiss and then she tottered around on the spot, manoeuvring her frame as she went, and shuffled up the hallway to the front room, as I closed the front door behind us.

A couple of weeks before I started working with Jill I had been to Age Concern for an interview. I had often thought about doing voluntary work while the children were little and before I started working. I had also read a Jehovah's Witness article which said that for people in a state of unhappiness or depression it was good to keep busy doing things for others, in order to prevent feelings of self-pity and it quoted Philippians 2:4 which says "Each of you should look not only to your own interests, but also to the interests of others."

I have always felt drawn towards people who appear to be vulnerable and who need to be cared for. I have a soft spot for the elderly in particular. Elderly people, to me, have an endearing quality about them. Most of them that I come across are tastefully and neatly dressed, cheery and always game for a bit of banter. They come from a time when no one had much but they all made the most of what they did have. So when I left Honeywell I contacted Age Concern and went along for a chat – after that it was just a matter of waiting for them to contact me.

I began visiting Freda a few weeks after I started working with Jill. All I had to do was go and visit her for about an hour once a week, just to give her a bit of company. Freda was in her early eighties, her husand had passed away a few years earlier and she had no children. I found out later that she had gone down with peritonitis as a child and the treatment that she had undergone had left her unable to have children. She had no relatives living nearby and her friends had moved away from the neighbourhood over the years. Freda was unable to get to know her new neighbours as she could no longer get around without her walking frame and was consequently housebound. With her poor eyesight she was not able to cook for herself as she constantly burnt herself on the stove, so eventually a carer came in to wash her, dress her and fix her meals.

On my first few visits I would make us a cup of tea and we chatted and got to know each other. She was a wonderfully interesting person who had been born in and lived in Luton all her life. I love to hear about people and their lives and Freda was able to tell me all about Luton as it was in the old days. Luton is famous for its hat industry and car industry and Freda had worked at both at one time or another. It turns out that she had worked at the Vauxhall factory, where I had worked, during the Second World War sewing straps and buckles onto the tarpaulins of the big trucks.

She also had a roguish sense of humour and recounted funny stories that had us rolling around in fits of laughter. She told me about her husband, Fred, and their love of Boxer dogs and how one Christmas the tree chocolates kept on disappearing from the Christmas tree. Of course Freda had pointed an accusing finger at Fred but after Christmas she happened to spot something shiny sticking out from under the hearth rug in front of the fireplace, where the Christmas tree stood, so she pulled back one corner of the rug and found underneath a whole pile of chocolate wrappers. It seems that the dog had pulled the chocolates off the tree, snaffled them out of their wrappers and then pushed the wrappers under the rug.

After a while I began taking Freda out so that she could enjoy a change of scenery, we'd sling her walking frame in the back of my car and off we'd go. On one occasion we went to a nearby supermarket, where there is a little cafeteria on the premises, and bought ourselves some lunch. Freda ordered fish and chips and when it came along it was such a huge portion I thought to myself, "No little old lady with false teeth is ever going to get through that!" I couldn't believe my eyes when she proceeded to wolf down the whole lot! Afterwards, when I took her to do a bit of grocery shopping, she legged it down to the spirits aisle to buy herself a bottle of sherry.

We had many happy outings together, we explored different little pubs in the area and after enjoying a lovely meal we would contentedly cruise around in my car and Freda would quite often close her eyes and have a little doze.

One thing she wanted to do more than anything was to go and visit Fred's grave, so one lovely summer's day I drove her to the beautiful little church yard and got down on my knees and cleared all the weeds from around the grave while Freda sat on a sunny bench nearby. I had such a feeling of peace, companionship and the sort of contentment that comes from doing something really worthwhile. When she died I felt overwhelmed with gratitude to God for His gift – for the wonderful privilege of knowing her for a little while and especially at that time in her life when she really needed somebody.

She passed away in February 2004 after suffering a bad fall, and is buried in the same plot as her beloved Fred. During the course of our friendship Freda had told me so much about her life but I, on the other hand, had told her very little about mine nor did I ever let her know that I struggled with depression. For the first time in my life I had a relationship with someone which existed purely for the benefit of that person, and where my needs held a place of no importance. It is a relationship that fills me with joy every time I think about it and it is one that I will always treasure. I experienced how it feels to give to someone without wanting anything in return and I witnessed how it is possible to think positively and be cheerful, just as Freda did, when there seems not much to be cheerful about.

Through my relationships with Jill and Freda, God helped me to see how it is possible to help other people and in the simplest of ways. What a wonderful privilege it is, when I look back, to be able to help someone through the most difficult time of their life. After Jill died I became a volunteer for Hospice at Home and now I visit people who are terminally ill and who prefer to remain in the comfort of their own homes. Our visits allow the main carers time for themselves, which was so valuable to Jill's mother for instance, to give her a break from a very demanding and intense situation. It also gives the client or the client's family or the carer an opportunity to talk about the situation to someone outside of the family who is not emotionally involved. It is an outlet for their grief and their fears and an opportunity for us to be able to *listen*, mostly, and where appropriate to comfort and encourage. I believe that it is always possible to help others, no matter what situation we may be in ourselves. In my daily readings there was a story about a lady who was housebound and confined to a wheelchair who began a ministry in helping people over the telephone, for anyone who needed a listening ear.

When I was isolated I felt like I must be the only person in the world with problems and my mind was consumed with thoughts about myself, my problems and my family. Now I think of all those whom I care about and about their welfare and the less I think about myself the happier I feel. Also, it keeps my problems in perspective. I pray for people constantly and, therefore, so often experience the joy of answered prayer.

The best way to help yourself is to help another.

William Horwood

Let us endeavour so to live that when we
come to die even the undertaker will be
sorry.

Mark Twain

I slept and dreamt that life was all joy, I awoke and understood life was but service; I served and realised service is joy.

Sir Rabindranath Tagore

The Workplace

I have to be honest with you, if I were to I walk into a room full of people and perhaps saw someone who looked miserable on one side of the room and someone who was laughing and joking on the other side of the room, my natural inclination would be to head towards the cheerful looking person. I'm sure I speak for all of us when I say that this is human nature, people are just people and nobody is perfect. That was a lesson that I learned many years ago. You may be going through a terrible time and you might be aching inside but people are not mind readers, and they are quick to judge you on your outside appearance. It is no good getting upset with people and thinking that it's unfair because, if we were in their shoes, we would more than likely respond in the same way. A visible injury or disability is easy to spot and sympathise with, but emotional pain is not.

This is the same in the workplace. I used to go into work day after day feeling wretched, much of the time it took all I had to make myself get out of bed, get ready and go. But what I learned to do was to 'act happy'. You can't take your personal problems into the workplace, you can't take them out on other people and you can't bring other people down – it's not fair on them. Many people find it hard enough going to work day in and day out, and other people have problems too.

I often used to drive into the car park at work, stop the engine and then sit gripping the steering wheel for a couple of seconds, then I would take a deep breath, get out of the car and walk into the office. As I got through the office door I would switch on my 'happy face' and greet everyone cheerily as I walked to my desk. My fondness of the people that I worked with and my interest in them helped to make my cheerful countenance more genuine, after all I was unhappy because of my problems, not because of them. I still struggled even after I had come out of my depression because my problems didn't miraculously disappear, it's just that God had equipped me with the strength to be able to handle them, and the period of time before Jill died was an ordeal to get through.

At a couple of places where I worked I was blessed to have someone to confide in. I made a point of not going around telling everyone my problems – I had made this mistake in the past also and had learned from it. As I said before, people are only human, and if you go around all the time looking miserable and telling people all your problems they tend to get bored and start avoiding you – and who can blame them? The best thing, I found, was to find someone at work that I could confide in, someone whom I felt I could trust not to talk about my problems all over the office, and the same applied outside of the office – I had a small group of two or three close friends whom I trusted and whom I could confide in but apart from that I kept my problems to myself.

Because I was struggling so much of the time because of my depression I tried also to only talk about problems to these close friends when it was really bad and not let myself be miserable all the time because that is tough, even on the best of friends. I made sure, by the way I conducted myself and by allowing my sense of humour to surface whenever possible, that my friends could see that I was a worthwhile person to stick with during the rough times, and this way I developed for myself a little support group. At work, if I came into work struggling with a particular problem, I would have a quick chat with my friend and get it off my chest and then I would get my head down and get on with my day's work. For a start getting it off my chest helped me to be able to focus on the job and concentrate a little easier. After a while a natural enjoyment of my colleagues' company, and to a great extent my work, would cause my spirits to begin to lift. On rare occasions, when a particular incident outside of work had really upset me, nothing could lift my spirits and I would sit quietly working, feeling as heavy as a lump of concrete and literally drag myself around the office. On these days I would feel so bad – but feel incapable of doing anything about it – because I could sense that the others were also subdued and I would feel so fed up with myself that I had succeeded in bringing them down too. It would also have the effect of sapping my confidence and I didn't perform so well at my job whereas when I managed to laugh and joke my way through the day I felt that I was handling the day successfully and this would boost my confidence and I would cope with the workload a lot better and I could work well.

One thing that helped me an awful lot was to make sure that I prayed first thing in the morning. I would pray to God to please give me the strength to work hard and put in a good day's work. (This was once I had started praying again). Then I would feel armed and prepared for the day and could approach it with confidence.

How I conducted myself at work was important to me. How the boss viewed me and my work was important to me. Mainly because I am a Christian and I wanted to set a good example and glorify God but also because, for all I knew, I was going to struggle with depression for the rest of my life and I wanted to show that, even though I had a problem, I was not a sap and that I had guts. Many people in life suffer from illness or pain and many grit their teeth and get on with it without complaining and they hold down jobs and are good workers, and that's the way I wanted to be viewed. I never wanted to use my depression as an excuse. I once heard a story about two people who were discussing an acquaintance who had died. During the course of the conversation it was revealed that one of the pair had never realised that this person had suffered from depression all his life, because of the way that he had conducted himself. That was what I wanted people to be able to say about me. I worked hard and did my best at work, right from my first job in South Africa, working steadily and with accuracy. I was always blessed with much recognition of my effort, always receiving good increases and generous bonuses. My bosses were always very good to me even on a personal level – at my job in South Africa, if I worked overtime, my boss would pay for my husband and myself to go out to dinner on his expense account. I still keep in touch with David, my boss from the development company, and we are good friends.

I made a point not getting involved in company politics – for one thing because it all seemed very petty – and I tried very hard not to get involved in gossip, which was not always easy because I found it hard to resist. I wanted people to know that I had integrity and that I was not one to talk behind people's backs. After all trust had always been a big issue in my life and there was no point in wanting people whom I could trust if I was not trustworthy myself. I also handled people with courtesy and treated them with a proper respect.

I have always found working hard and conducting myself in good manner to be satisfying. Not everything I did was interesting to me, every job had its boring tasks but because I worked to do them well regardless I still found them enjoyable to a certain extent. I feel that this is something very valuable – that it contributed towards my healing – a feeling of self-worth and self-respect that I had striven to earn.

My job is real work, and real work is play, not drudgery.

Madeline L'Engle

Whatever you do, work at it with all your heart,
as working for the Lord, not for men.

Colossians 3:23

The reward of a thing well done is to have done it. –

Ralph Waldo Emerson

One of my favourite mottos

People forget how fast you did a job –
but they remember how well you did it.

Howard Newton

I agree with this whole heartedly – it seems today that although there is never enough time to do a job properly, there is always time to go back and fix mistakes

Attitude can make a dynamic difference. The right attitude really can help you see the grind as a game. It can help your stress level drop and your life grow simpler and more peaceful. Every job has elements of drudgery. Every job has elements you like less than others. But I truly believe that almost any task can offer a measure of enjoyment if it is approached with the right spirit.

Thomas Kinkade

Tim Sanders, in his book *Likeability Factor*, says that a person who provides others with a 'sense of joy, happiness, relaxation, or rejuvenation' is more likely to be hired or promoted.

ODB

There are two different types of people: those who come into a room and say "Well, here I am!" – and those who come in and say "Ah. There you are!"

Anon

"Let your light shine before men, that they may see your good deeds and praise your Father in heaven."

Matthew 5:16

The moon reflects the sun and moves the oceans of the world with its gravitational pull and yet it can sometimes go unnoticed as it quietly lights up the night sky. In the same way we can quietly go about our lives but influence people by the way in which we conduct ourselves.

ODB

No coffee, no workee!

Just a bit on nonsense – I spotted this on a fridge magnet

Lead a Simple Existence

In late 2005 several opportunities arose for outreach in the community that I was eager to be a part of and as things at the office hadn't been the same since Jill died it felt like a good time to move on, so in December 2005 I resigned.

Instead, I had saved up and as my son and daughter finished at school I paid for them to fly out to South Africa so that they could spend a couple of months with their Grandparents and cousins before they started at college. This was something special that I, personally, wanted to do for them to encourage them to work hard at school and because it was clear that they had suffered similar loss to what I have experienced in life in leaving loved ones behind when we had moved back to England. Apart from this, it was also important to me to treat the children in the way that I would have liked to have been treated by my Mum and I knew that the nature of this gift would show them just how much they mean to me. I had also saved up and brought another of my closest friends over to England, from South Africa, for Christmas the year that Jill died. Terry had been so good and generous to us over the years when my husband was unemployed, giving us so much encouragement, and it was an opportunity to be able to give back. We had such a blast and she has very fond memories of her English Christmas with us.

In the New Year I began helping my schoolteacher friend by cleaning her house once a week. It's a great mutual arrangement where her weekend is free of housework and I have a little pocket money.

> Keep your lives free from the love of money and
> be content with what you have.
>
> *Proverbs 13:5*

I wanted to get more involved in community work, apart from my work as a volunteer for Hospice at Home, and there were a couple of outreach projects on the go. As a volunteer for Hospice at Home I began doing visits and quite often attend training sessions on different topics. My first client past away recently but as with Freda and Jill I felt so privileged to have known her for a little while – she was a lovely, cheerful and uncomplaining soul who spent most of her life helping others – and to be of help in a small way, mainly by just listening to her, during the most difficult time of her life. These sorts of experiences help you to see life and its difficulties in a proper perspective, and have the effect of making you feel extremely grateful for all that you have.

I remember days when I used to sit in church and the pastor would tell us that we are called to be disciples of God. I remember thinking that I would never be able to teach anyone anything. I believed that that was what the ministry was there for, not ordinary people like you and me. I can't believe what I am involved in now, I honestly cannot believe that I am the same person. For one thing I am writing this book and if I hadn't experienced all that I've been through I wouldn't have anything to write about, I could never take the step to obey God's call to try to help others with their problems without going through the same problems myself.

One of our outreach projects involves going into schools (at the moment we are at the local junior school) and teaching the children about God's word by acting out Bible stories. We are known to the school and the children as the 'Storytellers' and we mostly follow the stories set out in the Storyteller Bible, a series called 'Open The Book.' We act out stories such as *David and Goliath, Daniel in the Lion's Den* and – one that makes me chuckle – *Jonah the Groaner.* Now, if you'd told me years ago that one day I would be acting out Bible stories in front of a bunch of school children and their teachers I would have said "No way!" Not going to work gives me the opportunity to do this and I can't tell you how much I enjoy it, the children look forward to us coming (what child doesn't enjoy a story?) and even one or two of the teachers have told us that they enjoy our performances and look forward to us coming. It's a great way to overcome self-consciousness as we don't have a critical audience. We go once a fortnight and we begin by recapping the story from the previous visit and when we ask the children questions they remember so much. One day when they are older they might look back fondly on those days and if they go through a particular difficulty maybe their memories will bring to mind a story that might be able to help them through it.

Our church services are held on Saturdays at the local Methodist Church hall which we rent from them. They worship on Sundays so it is a good arrangement. We quite often get involved in combined events such as the luncheon club which we run for the elderly once a month. We have a team of cooks who are paired off and who take it in turns to cook, each pair cooks about once a quarter. In January I signed up and now help to cook meals catering for thirty people. My specialities are cottage pie and lasagne. The lunches are very popular and we now have our regulars who turn up each time, it gives the elderly folk a chance to meet and have some company while they enjoy a lovely home cooked meal which they have not had to prepare for themselves. Transport is also provided for those who need it.

The Pastor of the Methodist Church, Betty, left recently in order to go into full time ministerial training and has been replaced by someone who oversees several congregations so cannot be involved in the various activities to the same extent that Betty was. Betty used to live in the residence attached to the church. She used to provide the transport for the luncheon club, she used to hold a Bible study for the elderly at one of their Homes called Bethune and she was community governor at the school where we do 'Open The Book.' I have taken over the transporting of the elderly to the luncheon club and to Bethune, I assist our pastor's wife in leading the Bible study which is also a monthly event, and I have taken over the role of community governor at the school so have to attend various meetings regarding the welfare of the school. Our church has set up a local community website on the Internet and it is my responsibility to gather information from the local community centre and other sources, concerning local events going on in our community for the website. The sense of community that I have developed through being involved in so many projects has given me a wonderful sense of stability, which is a very real gift after all the moving I have done over the years.

There are four elderly ladies whom I transport regularly and they are an absolute pleasure. They are so grateful to be able to get out of their houses and have some company and never hesitate to tell me so. One of the ladies is housebound like Freda was and from day to day has no visitors with the exception of her daughter, who is very good to her. I recently found out that the pub in a nearby village holds lunches once a week for the elderly and charge next to nothing for a three course meal, so as there are no events on for a couple of weeks in the month I now take my four ladies out to lunch there once a month.

I can appreciate that this lifestyle may not suit everyone but I experience a tremendous amount of joy and satisfaction from what I do. My life is very busy but I'm busy doing things that I enjoy and which I feel are worthwhile. I recently read a biography of Mother Theresa's life of service and was so moved that I felt inspired to emulate the Sisters of Charity who live frugally but give generously of their time and their love. All those whom they help they treat as if they were serving Jesus, according to scripture (Matthew 25:40). I am constantly juggling my finances and pray continually for help, however I always seem to have enough and the family has enough – things always work out.

I am blessed with a wonderful feeling of peace. It is a peace that comes from trusting God completely, obeying His will to the best of my ability and putting my life in His hands. I am very fortunate that God has blessed me with a generous spirit and I have always found a lot of pleasure in giving to people and charities. As a result of this, when I left work I put our family finances in God's hands and prayed to Him saying, "You have said that it is better to give than to receive, and this I have done because of the generous spirit which You have put in me. Now I claim your promise that You will look after my family as I strive to obey You and fulfil what I believe is Your purpose for me - to teach Your word and give hope and encouragement to others." I don't know what the future holds but whatever it is I have peace that all is in God's hands and I live each day confidently.

I strive to live an unmaterialistic, uncluttered, simple existence that is balanced, structured and orderly. 'God is not a God of confusion, but of peace and order' (1 Corinthians 14:33). I recognise and accept my limitations, I don't overcommit myself and I have learned to be firm and say 'no' as an act of self-preservation. I find also that it helps to use a planner to make a note of all that needs to be done. In this way I feel I have better control of my life and gain a great deal of satisfaction from ticking things off my list daily. If there is an item that I have not been able to get to I will cross it off and slot it in on the next most suitable occasion. I've learned that if I give too much and stretch myself too thin I end up doing too many things and nothing well. It's important to conserve time and energy to give to things and people that really matter.

I believe that it's important to set realistic long and short term goals but also to try to be flexible – try to make the most of unexpected opportunities, especially when it comes to family. One Saturday, for example, I drove my husband to the airport and our teenage daughter came with us for the ride. It so happened that the route we took was through some beautiful English countryside and quaint little villages. It was lunchtime by the time we dropped my husband off so on the spur of the moment we decided to stop off and have lunch together at a little pub restaurant. It ended up being one of those rare and special moments between Mum and daughter that I will always treasure – we had a diet main course followed by the most wicked of puddings and we just sat and chatted about this and that. We eventually rolled out of there feeling pleasantly ill and in good humour.

Take the time to do simple little things that mean a lot. If it happened that I went shopping while the kids were at school and my husband at work I would always carefully lay out anything I'd bought for them on their beds so that when they got home at the end of the day they would find a little surprise.

I endeavour to enjoy each day moment by moment. I find that if I daydream excessively or spend much of my time lost in thought about things such as past events or thinking about what needs to be done in the future that I lose out on the present, especially when I'm driving I can become so absorbed in my thoughts that

I miss out on many beautiful scenes. I consciously keep a control of my mind and my thoughts so that I can make the most of what is going on here and now. This enables me to live each day fully.

A ROSE IN A BOTTLE

Behold the lilies of the field;
Solomon in all his glory
Was not arrayed as one of these.

And behold a rose
Not in a garden
Or in some florist's artfully bound bouquet,
But in a bottle
A milk bottle in a kitchen
With the sounds of the dishes,
The radio and the children at breakfast.
A rose in a bottle
Startling among the cereals and the marmalade,
As if in the midst of our domestic reality
A greater reality had sprung up
Between the salt and pepper and the butter dish.

Through the window is the garden,
Leaves and grass and roses.
Outside the window,
Beyond the cat washing his ears,
Is the garden I have seen so often
And yet so often do not see.
But this single flower

This rose in a bottle
Demands my attention.

Each velvet smooth petal
Softly curved and rounded,
Each subtle change of colour
From leaf and stem
To the depth of its bloom
Draws me closer
Until I am bewitched by the fragrance
That belongs to only this particular flower.
And there it stands between teapot and toast
Telling me that today
I shall not see anything more beautiful.

Lord
Let me not be blind
To the beauty I will see today.
Let me see the beauty
That I usually ignore
In people.
In between the queues for buses and trains,
In between the telephone calls
And the voices of friends and colleagues
Let me see beauty,
In words spoken with thought and care
In a job well done
In a single gesture of kindness.

Today You have shown me the beauty of a rose

In a bottle,

In an ordinary kitchen.

Let me see also the flower of love

That you have planted in ordinary people.

Frank Topping

I now have proper time to keep my home clean and tidy and to prepare good meals, as well as have time to myself, and I find this very satisfying.

It is the simple things of life that make living worthwhile,

the sweet fundamental things such as love and duty, work

and rest and living close to nature.

Laura Ingalls Wilder

An important change in my life is that even though it is still hectic I can now rest when I need to. I once read that we need to step off the treadmill and have regular periods of rest. We cannot push ourselves to keep on going day in and day out, we need a good balance of work combined with rest. I find that when my life gets out of kilter I lose perspective.

Tiredness is very closely linked to depression and when I get tired I feel down, so I make sure I take the time to sit in my favourite armchair and read or watch the birds outside or doze, constantly recharging my batteries throughout the day. It wasn't easy to do this when I was at work so I had to try to structure my free time well - allow myself a little nap on Sunday afternoons and sometimes go out for take-aways to give myself a break from cooking. One thing I have always done is kept the Sabbath. The Sabbath, whichever day you choose to observe it, is a very necessary day of rest which I believe God commanded us to keep for a good reason.

> If you're working hard to make a living,
> Never taking time to smell the roses,
> Now's the time to heed the Bible's wisdom:
> Find true joy before your life's day closes.
>
> *Hess*

The first thing I like to do every morning when I get up is to open the curtains of our upstairs landing window, which faces east, to look at the sunrise. No two sunrises are ever the same but they are all breathtaking and if it is raining outside and the sky is full of clouds it is still beautiful. Our back yard is west facing and the sitting room is always light and airy. In the afternoon the sun shines in directly through the patio doors and when a pool of sunlight reaches my favourite armchair I like to sit there and doze. Then as the day draws to a close we are privy to some of the most amazing sunsets.

MORNING LIGHT

Looking through a window
With sleepy morning eyes
I saw an artist at work.
The early light
Tingeing sky pink and rose
Struggled through mist and cloud
And bathed my mundane view in mystery.
Rooftops glistening, wet with morning dew
Glowed with brief reflected glory.

In the miracle of the morning
Back garden sheds,
Victorian bricks and sash windows
Are dressed in borrowed finery;
A precious gift from the rising winter sun,
A fleeting prize that must be captured
Before the greyness over-rules.

Beneath the rafters of every suburban house
Alarm clocks rattle, kettles boil
And razors fight their endless battle
With bearded chins,
Unaware of unheralded majesty
Passing silent overhead.
Days begin with breakfast
And the Lord of life
Waits without acknowledgement.

Lord of the heavens
Your light transforms
The skylines of cities and towns.
Forgive me for those days
In which the morning paper
And the wireless news
Take precedence over You.
Each and every day
You offer me the miracle of Your love,
A loving presence
That can transform my life

If only I could be still

For long enough to receive Your gift.

Lord, each morning

Open my eyes

And let me live

In the light of Your love.

Frank Topping

SKY

Lord of life

There is no part of Your creation

That does not speak of the wonder of Your being.

Day by day

We walk and laugh and live

Beneath the changing endless sky.

In cities, in the countryside,

Or beyond the land

Where sea and sky marry

In mysterious union of height and depth,

Reflecting moon and stars and rising sun

When those with ears can hear

The sons of morning singing for joy.

And yet, how often have I missed

The songs of heaven,

With eye and mind tuned only

To morning news

And the fleeting hands of clocks.

Beneath the dome of heaven
The sky continues her dance
With shapes and changing colour.
From first light to dawn
The world is created once again from darkness.
Out of mists and shadows
The sun in splendour beyond the reach of kings
Breathes life into the world.
His feathered cirrostratus train trails
Aloof to robust cumulus running before the bustle
Of the south-west wind.
And in the night
Stars stand sentinel until dawn.
Moonlight caresses hills, ships
And dreaming lovers
In the endless, everchanging drama
Played above the heads of people
Boarding trains, washing cars,
Buying, selling, sleeping unaware
Of imprisonment
Or the snare of smaller things.

Lord of all created things
Let me lift up my eyes just once this day.
May the passing problems of my waking hours
Be reduced to their proper size and place
Beneath the infinite sky.
May I know your presence,

Feel and breathe the breath of life
Which is your daily gift,
And may I see
In the beauty of the heavens
The measure of your love.

Frank Topping

The Lord said to Moses, "Speak to the Israelites and say to them: 'Throughout the generations to come you are to make tassels on the corners of your garments, with a blue cord on each tassel. You will have these tassels to look at and so you will remember all the commandments of the Lord, that you may obey them.

Numbers 15:37 – 39

The blue thread – the colour of the heavens above – spoke of God's immeasurable power and saving grace

ODB

God manifests Himself to us through His creation and this brings peace to our souls in just as absorbing His word does. Just looking out into my back garden at the grass, shrubs, hedges, trees and sky brings me peace. We have a little robin redbreast in our garden and on wintry days when the trees and hedges are bare and the sky is a dull grey the robin is a little flash of red as he flits around in the hedge. On the odd occasion when I'm feeling a bit blue he always seems to appear from nowhere and the sight of him lifts my spirits. I can always hear him outside making his nasal peeping or zick-zick noises and in spring the lilting and trilling of the blackbirds can be heard from all different parts of the garden as they flit from one perch to another. The first sign of spring is always the daffodil shoots protruding through the soil of the flower beds, at first just barely visible and then more and more so until suddenly the beds are filled with the riotous yellow of nodding daffodils. A sight to make your heart sing.

> Drop Your still dews of quietness,
>
> till all our strivings cease;
>
> take from our souls
>
> the strain and stress
>
> and let our ordered lives confess
>
> the beauty of Your peace.
>
> Breathe through the heats of our
>
> desire
>
> Your coolness and Your balm,
>
> Let sense be dumb, let flesh
>
> retire,
>
> Speak through the earthquake,
>
> wind, and fire,
>
> O still small voice of calm!
>
> *Mission Praise 111*

I never tire of the daily journey to and from my daughter's school. The school driveway is long as it runs parallel to the sports fields and it is lined on both sides by all different types of trees – oaks, elms, birches and ashes amongst others. In springtime the trees are full of shoots and then leaves that are tender and green and they, along with the clumps of daffodils that grow along the sides of the roads between our house and the school, herald the fact that another winter is over and that summer is just around the corner. Then in autumn the leaves turn beautiful vivid reds

and oranges and a bite in the air tells us that the Christmas season
is on its way.

FIELDS

It's just a field
An English field in summer.
Beneath my head is grass,
Green and cloverleaf.
In my eyes and on my face
Dappled shadows,
Sunlight filtered through leaves of silver birch
Shimmering on a gentle breeze.
In my ears, the sounds of insects,
Grasshoppers, crickets,
Dragonflies and bees
Humming and hovering in heat and haze,
Exploring the hearts of flowers
Wild and sturdy in the hedgerows.
And in my head
The scent of fresh cut grass
Soothing the intrusive thoughts
Of a mind that never rests.
And it's just a field
An English field in summer.

A county, surrounded by mist grey hills,
Stretches like a patchwork quilt
Of greens and browns and golds
Stitched by hedges and lanes,
Decorated with cattle and sheep,
Knotted together with whitewalled cottages,
Farmyards and barns.
Deep, rural, harvest seedbeds
Pushing up from rain-rich soil,
Grain, corn, barley, oats and hay,
Filling the shelves of the supermarkets,
The pantries of the suburban semis.

Bread on the breakfast table.

Yet not by bread alone shall we live
Here in this field
Like the wind playing with the grass
Blows the Spirit.
The Spirit that brought forth the world
From the void of space,
The breath of life that feeds me
So that I shall never hunger.
In this very breath that I breathe
Is the mystery of all created things,
In this field
This English field in summer.

Frank Topping

It's no secret that human beings can find healing and restoration through contact with nature. It's no secret that growing things soothe the mind,

that wild things uplift the soul, that rocks and hills and trees do something undefinable but positive for the human spirit.

Thomas Kinkade

A VISION OF CHILDREN

I dream'd I saw a little brook

Run rippling down the Strand;

With cherry-trees and apple-trees

Abloom on either hand:

The sparrows gathered from the squares,

Upon the branches green;

The pigeons flock'd from Palace-yard,

Afresh their wings to preen;

And children down St. Martin's Lane,

And out of Westminster,

Came trooping many a thousand strong,

With a bewilder'd air.

They hugged each other round the neck,

And titter'd for delight,

To see the yellow daffodils,

And see the daisies white;

They rolled upon the grassy slopes,

And drank the water clear,

While buses the Embankment took,

Ashamed to pass a-near;

And sandwich-men stood still aghast,

And costermongers smiled;

And a policeman on his beat

Pass'd weeping like a child.

Thomas Ashe

To sit and read my Bible, first thing in the morning, is without a doubt essential for starting a successful day. Quietly reading God's word fills me with peace and prepares me for the day ahead. It focuses my mind on what is important and it gives me a positive start.

"Be still, and know that I am god."
Psalm 46:10
A quiet place helps us listen to God.

Mum

Mum and I had been estranged and I knew she'd moved away to a place by the sea. When I was in my thirties though I received a letter from Mum with a stamped self-addressed envelope asking if we could be reconciled but because I was still struggling with my marriage and depression I felt I couldn't cope with her so did not reply and threw the letter in the bin. Sometime later, after I'd finished at work and had been doing my voluntary work for a couple of years, and I was more mature and not so hot headed, I thought about Mum and wondered to myself whether she would enjoy going on outings with me. I had such fun with my old lady friends going here and there and I thought maybe Mum and I could become good friends and have lots of fun so I set about tracing her as I didn't have her address. I couldn't find her in any directories so I asked The Salvation Army family tracing service to find her for me but they came back to me sometime later and said that she'd died and had been dead a couple of years. She'd died of bronchial pneumonia and her ashes had been scattered out to sea from a RNLI lifeboat as she had been a supporter of them. Her husband didn't inform us of her death or her funeral even though he had my contact details but I hardly knew him so I wasn't really surprised.

Anyway, it was a horrible shock to myself and my brother. I would never have a chance to tell her that I was sorry for my part in our falling out and I'd never be able to tell her that I love her. No matter what, she was my Mum. Somewhere along the way in her life she'd been affected so that she couldn't relate to me or talk to me but as I got older and was taking my old lady friends out I knew I didn't so much need a Mum anymore. The important thing was for me to be a good Mum to my kids. But I so wanted to be a best friend to her and love her like she'd never been loved her whole life.

One day my husband took me to see the place where she'd lived before her death. We bought a bouquet of flowers and I took a copy of the poem Invictus laminated and we threw them out to sea and had our own little farewell so that I could have some closure. My husband left me alone so that I could have a while with her by myself. There's a sailors' church on the harbour close to where the RNLI operate from and Mum's name is printed with a list of others who have died and whose ashes have been scattered like Mum's were, on a notice board outside the church. I've also paid a donation for one of the new life boats to be named after my Mum. Seldom a day goes by that I don't think about her and miss her so the love that I can't express to her is being expressed here in this book in this moment instead.

The seaside town in Kent, England where she lived has become our favourite place to go hiking along the coast. The weather there always seems to be beautiful no matter what is going on in the rest of the country and I feel at peace there and close to Mum.

Death

Just before Jill died I had a dream. I dreamt I was in heaven. My heaven consisted simply of an ordinary English street with a row of terraced houses running up either side. In my dream I was walking up the street, it was a beautiful sunny day, and as I walked past each house, in every tiny little front garden, busily working with spades and trowels, weeding, digging and tidying, were people whom I love. But they were those people who have either passed away or whom, for one reason or another, I no longer have contact with. Jill was there, my Mum, my grandparents and many others, and as I made my way up the street I stopped at each house, leant over the gate and had a little chat with each individual and we stood there at the gate talking and laughing and nodding to one another amiably.

I've experienced a great deal of loss in my life, from moving from place to place and changing jobs and through the death of people whom I care about. Losing people and having to say goodbye through the years has caused me much heartache. I believe that my dream symbolised the reunion and reconciliation that will occur in the future when Jesus Christ returns. My belief and absolute trust in God's promise, has given me the sort of comfort, peace and hope for the future that is hard for me to express. The Bible says that we should store up for ourselves 'treasures in heaven' (Matt 6:19 –21; Luke 12:32 – 34) and God knows that, for me personally, treasures have nothing to do with silver or gold or material possessions, but rather reconciliation and reunion with the ones that I love. Only God could know the enormous value of gift that He was giving, in that any future loss would be a little easier for me to bear as I would only have to picture that loved one in my 'heaven' and I would feel comforted, as I did when Jill died and as I do when I think about my mum and that fact that one day we will have another chance. This has been one of the greatest contributing factors to my healing.

Brothers, we do not want you to be ignorant about those who fall asleep, or to grieve like the rest of men, who have not hope. We believe that Jesus died and rose again and so we believe that God will bring with Jesus those who have fallen asleep in Him.

1 Thess 4:13 & 14

In 1991, famed British guitarist Eric Clapton was stricken with grief when his 4-year-old son Conor died as a result of a fall from an apartment window. Looking for an outlet for his grief, Clapton penned perhaps his most poignant ballad: 'Tears In Heaven'. It seems that every note weighs heavy with the sense of pain and loss that can be understood only by a parent who has lost a child.

Surprisingly, however, Clapton said in a television interview years later, "In a sense, it wasn't even a sad song. **It was a song of belief. When it [says that] there will be no more tears in heaven, I think it's a song of optimism – of reunion.**" [Emphasis mine.]

THE COMPANY OF HEAVEN

How many years had I looked
At sandstone rocks, red and soft,
Scoured by wind,
Engraved with lovers' initials and dates,
And never noticed that the earth beneath the grass
Was the same rich red.

I saw its redness that day,
Felt its coarse dryness in my hands
As we stood around and prayed.
Prayed with the wind in our faces
For the passing of my father.
The voice of the priest
Mingled with the breeze and birdsong
But in my head was the music of memory,
Voices, songs, stories
Sounding again and again in my mind,
And I knew
That he was not there,
Not beneath the flowers,
Not beneath the gaze of our bowed heads,
And yet he was with us
As he had never been before.
He, his brothers and his sisters
And all the company of heaven

Reassuring us of a promise fulfilled.

In My father's house are many mansions
And I go to prepare a place for you
So that where I am, you may be also;
If it were not so I would have told you.
And suddenly, in my mind's eye, I saw them,
Two tromboning brothers
Laughing whilst counting the rest bars
In the music of eternity.

The refrain was familiar
Yet I could not catch the tune,
And knew I never would
Not as long as I stood here
Or walked the journey of my days.
But the words, I knew,
At least the prelude to that unfinished masterpiece
Whose opening chorus begins,
The eye has not seen
Nor the ear heard,
Nor has it entered the heart of man
What things have been prepared
For those who love god.

And there
With that red earth beneath my feet,
I knew
That nothing could separate me

From the love of Christ

Or the love of those

Whose song, even now,

Is singing in my soul.

Frank Topping

Why Does God Allow Suffering?

There was a time when thinking about the suffering that goes on in this world was enough in itself to perpetuate my depression. My mind would often wander to those in different parts of the world who were suffering, and suffering to such a horrific extent that it made my unhappiness seem trifling. It even occurred to me that with this realisation, surely, I could jump start myself out of my depression, but without real answers and - at the time when I was no longer praying - without God, I was going nowhere. Pictures would flash through my mind of, here, a child crying pitifully from being abused and, there, a poor homeless person sleeping rough in a dark and wet alley. It filled me with grief to think of people starving in third world countries, children suffering from being caught up in war in places like Sierra Leone and women and children being used as sex slaves in different parts of the world. The daily news did nothing to dispel this grim aspect and what made it worse was to think that many of these things were also going on my back doorstep.

I thought long and hard before I eventually decided to get involved in voluntary work as I was concerned that I would get too emotionally involved and may even turn out to be no good at helping anyone, which would have knocked my confidence even further. Besides, for every person that I may try to help weren't there a million others out there in the same position? Would this lead me to further feelings of hopelessness? But this question was answered when I read Mother Theresa's biography. She said that if she dwelled on those who she wasn't able to reach she would have become totally demoralised so she concentrated on putting her all into helping whomsoever she could.

I used to question God, asking Him "What is it that You want from us?"

One Sunday, God led me to the Luton Christian Fellowship Church – the church that one of the Christians that I worked with attended – where I received an answer that turned my mind around. The speaker explained how God lives a perfect existence that is incredible beyond anything the human mind could ever conceive. Far from wanting anything *from* us, God wants us to participate in that existence or state of holiness *with* Him. That is what He wants *for* us. We were told that what once stood between us and that existence was our sinful human state and that if we entered God's holiness taking our imperfections with us we would have the effect of corrupting it, "Flesh and blood cannot inherit the Kingdom of God, nor does the perishable inherit the imperishable." Hebrews 12:10 says "God disciplines us for our good, that we may share in His holiness" and verse 14 says "Make every effort to live in peace with all men and be holy; without holiness no-one will see the Lord." That is why we had to be saved and made holy and perfect by the death of His Son, Jesus Christ through a process called justification whereby Jesus lived and died and rose again to restore our relationship with God. Justification means being put right with God.

Jesus died so that what was imperfect was made perfect or what was 'perishable' has been made 'imperishable'. Through His death and resurrection He has made it possible for us to enter the presence of God.

To try to understand why God allows suffering it helps, first of all, to understand how *God* feels about suffering. The only real source we have today to enable us to do this is the Bible. Through its prophecies the New Testament helps us to understand what is taking place in the world today. In the Old Testament a very similar situation took place and it describes God's feelings and reactions to all that went on. It tells us in Malachi 3:6 "I the Lord do not change" and in the New Testament we are told "Jesus Christ is the same yesterday and today and for ever." What God felt about what went on in biblical times is the same as what He feels when He sees what goes on *today*. This gives us a clear insight as to how God feels about the *suffering* that goes on in the world today.

God's infinite purpose has *always* been to share eternal life, not with robots – who are *programmed* to obey - but with intelligent, free thinking beings. He wanted people to *choose* to obey Him. In the Old Testament, Abraham proved to be very much the sort of being God was looking for – Abraham chose to obey God, therefore God chose to use Abraham for a very specific purpose. He blessed Abraham's wife (who was unable to have children) with a son, whom they were to name Isaac, in order that their line could be continued. Later, as an ultimate test of his obedience to God, God asked Abraham to sacrifice Isaac to Him. At the last minute, just as Abraham was about to take Isaac's life, God commanded him not to "lay a hand on the boy." God then established a covenant with Abraham and He promised a blessing on his descendants forever (Genesis 12:1-3). Isaac married and had a son called Jacob, whose name was changed to Israel (Genesis 35:10). Jacob had twelve sons whose descendants became known as the 'children of Israel'.

During a time of famine in the land of Canaan the Israelites had gone to settle in Egypt where the Pharaoh who was ruling at the time treated them fairly. However the Pharaoh who succeeded him as ruler felt threatened by the now large numbers of

Israelites populating his land and was worried that if a war broke out in Egypt the Israelites might side with the enemy against the Egyptians, so slave masters were put over them to oppress them with forced labour and they lived under a ruthless regime.

Eventually though God intervened and through Moses led the Israelites out of Egypt back to Canaan, The Promised Land. Even though God led them performing many miracles along the journey, He discovered that they were quick to grumble and complain as soon as anything didn't go their way and once in the Promised Land they soon began to turn their backs on God. They requested a human king and leader instead of looking solely to God for rulership and they broke the covenant that God had established with their forefather, Abraham. Most offensive to God was that they began to worship manmade Gods and idols despite the fact that, in the book of Isaiah, God declared many times that *He* is God and that there are *no* others.

He implored the Israelites to turn from their evil ways and sent many prophets to warn them time and time again of what would happen if they did not but they continued to ignore Him completely. Eventually God allowed the Israelites to be taken back into captivity by the Babylonians for a period of time. God is slow to anger (Nahum 1:3) but He became enraged when He witnessed the perversions that were taking place amongst the Israelites and the sacrificing of their own children to their Gods and idols as referred to, for instance, in Jeremiah 32:28 – 35 "Therefore, this is what the Lord says: I am about to hand this city over to the Babylonians and to Nebuchadnezzar king of Babylon, who will capture it. The Babylonians who are attacking this city will come in and set it on fire; they will burn it down, along with the houses where the people provoked me to anger by burning incense on the roofs to Baal and by pouring out drink offerings to other Gods. The people of Israel and Judah have done nothing but evil in my sight from their youth; indeed, the people of Israel have done nothing but provoke me by all the evil they have done – they, their kings and officials, their priests and prophets, the men of Judah and the people of Jerusalem. They turned their backs to me and not their faces; though I taught them again and again, they would not listen or respond to discipline. They set up their abominable idols in the house that bears My name and defiled it. They built high places for Baal in the Valley of Ben Hinnom to sacrifice their sons and daughters to Molech, though I never commanded, nor did it enter My mind, that they should do such a detestable thing and so make Judah sin."

God gave the Israelites so much time, opportunity and warnings to change their ways, with promises of great rewards if they did, but they stubbornly refused to listen. Eventually in Ezekiel 5:9 God said, "Because of all your detestable idols, I will do to you what I have never done before and will never do again."

God did away with the old covenant because He knew that human nature rendered people incapable of living in total obedience. He then created a new covenant as Jeremiah 31:31 tells us, "I will make a new covenant with the house of Israel and with the house of Judah. It will not be like the covenant I made with their forefathers when I took them by the hand to lead them out of Egypt, because they broke My covenant..." Hebrews 6:18 also talks about the old covenant and its ineffectiveness saying "The former regulation is set aside because it was weak and useless (for the law made nothing perfect), and a better hope is introduced, by which we draw near to God." The new covenant comprised of the gift of salvation (we are rescued from death and given eternal life) by grace (God's gift of unearned forgiveness) and through faith in the death and resurrection of His son. Hebrews 6:22 tells us that "Jesus has become the guarantee of a better covenant." For those of us who might look at grace as being a loophole and question what there is to stop people from sinning if they know in advance that they will be forgiven, Philip Yancey - in his book 'What's So Amazing About Grace?' - explains this very effectively: "There is one 'catch' to grace that I must now mention. In the words of C. S. Lewis, *St. Augustine says 'God gives where He finds empty hands.' A man whose hands are full of parcels can't receive a gift.'* Grace, in other words, must be received….forgiveness needs to be accepted as well as offered if it is to be complete: and a man who admits no guilt can accept no forgiveness."

God shows us his love for the people of Israel in Jeremiah 31:3 "I have loved you with an everlasting love; I have drawn you with loving-kindness." He thought of them as being His people, "I will be their God, and they will be my people." (Jeremiah 31:33). When it became clear to God that the Israelites were not going to obey Him and He thought about the devastation and *suffering* that his people were about to bring on themselves because of their disobedience, He was agonised and broken hearted about it. Jeremiah, who had an insight into the grief that God was going through on behalf of His people, exclaims in chapter 4, "Oh, my anguish, my anguish! I writhe in pain. Oh, the agony of my heart!" Ezekiel 6:9 states, "How I have been grieved by their adulterous hearts."

Just as parents are loathe to punish their children but reluctantly do so after giving many, many warnings so was God loathe to punish the nation of Israel, but when He eventually did He did so fairly. "I will discipline you but only with justice" (Jeremiah 46:28).

Eventually, as He promised He would, after their period of punishment was over, God delivered those Israelites who had survived captivity (the remnant) from the hands of their oppressors and He forgave them, this time for eternity "for I will forgive the remnant I spare" (Jeremiah 50:20).

Today we live under the new covenant "an everlasting covenant that will not be forgotten" (Jeremiah 50:5), but this covenant includes *all* nations and *all* people, not only the descendants of Abraham. In the old testament God communicated with the people of the time through certain key characters and through the prophets. When Jesus was alive He chose disciples to represent Him knowing that He would only be on earth for a time, in Mark 16:15 & 16 He commanded, "Go into all the world and preach the good news to all creation. Whoever believes and is baptised will be saved, but whoever does not believe will be condemned." Christians today are under that same admonishment to go out and share the good news with as many people as possible before the return of Christ.

Just as in biblical times people are living lawless lives which causes much suffering in this world. Today's laws are based on the old testament law, the ten commandments, and these commandments were enforced to *benefit* people, to prevent people from bringing harm to each other as breaking the law only causes pain and heartache.

Many may wonder why someone had to *die* - why Jesus had to *die* - in order for us to be saved. Under the old covenant, if an individual broke the law he would have to pay a penalty (just as we have to today), in the form of a sacrifice, which was offered to God. It was required of him to select from his livestock only the *best* beasts, an action which would have caused him considerable personal loss, the equivalent of paying a large fine in today's terms. This system was only temporary because it showed itself to be ineffective in bringing an end to sin. In the New Testament God showed His love for mankind by willingly offering His Son,

Jesus, His most treasured possession, as the ultimate sacrifice for the sins of mankind, just as Abraham was prepared to offer up his beloved son, Isaac. Jesus was the only One who could meet God's demand for a perfect sacrifice – only He was sinless and because of this His death covered the sins of the whole world, there was no limit to the sin that His death could cover. (Hebrews 9:11 – 15) He provided the forgiveness of sins that sets us free and secures for us an eternal home in heaven as Hebrews 9:15 tells us. "Christ is the mediator of a new covenant, that those who are called may receive the promised eternal inheritance – now that He has died as a ransom to set them free from the sins committed under the first covenant."

It is prophesied in the Bible that before the end of this age many disasters are going to befall the world (Matthew 24). Many as a natural result of wrongdoing, such as the abuse of our planet, drugs, alcohol and sexual abuse. Just as God sent warnings to the Israelites to try and make them turn from their ways He is allowing events to take place which will one day open man's eyes to see that we cannot live without Him and that we need Him in our lives but, sadly, just as many people benefit from the rainfall that God sends from the sky (Matthew 5:45). (God is impartial – He loves us all the same) whether they be righteous or wrongdoers, so also many people suffer in bombings, plane crashes, wars and natural disasters no matter what their character might be. God has promised that when the right time comes – when people are willing to accept His leadership again after realising that human leadership is totally inadequate – He will intervene before humanity succeeds in annihilating itself completely.

In the meantime – just as anxious and loving parents, at times, have to restrain their natural instincts to protect their child and allow him to make mistakes, knowing that it is the only *real* way he is going to learn – God is watching all that is taking place in this world in absolute pain and anguish for mankind. Just as in old testament times, God is having to contend with our stubbornness and rebelliousness but even though this may prolong human suffering it gives an opportunity for as many people as possible to come to repentance (turn away from wrongs) as God wants *all* to be saved as we are told in 2 Peter 3:9 "The Lord is not slow in keeping His promise...He is patient with you, not wanting anyone to perish, but everyone to come to repentance." In Ezekiel 33:11 God says "As surely as I live, I take no pleasure in the death of the wicked, but rather that they turn from their ways and *live*." [Emphasis mine].

There is nothing we can do to make God love us more.

There is nothing we can do to make God love us less.

Philip Yancey

God loves us because of who He is not because of who we are, His love is unconditional. He is kind and merciful, not someone who will put His arm around our shoulders one minute but punish us severely as soon as we step out of line.

Freedom is not the right to do what we want but the power to do what we ought.

Corrie Ten Boom

Live as free men, but do not use your freedom as a cover-up for evil; live as servants of God.

1 Peter 2:16

We are not children of the bondwoman but of the free.

Galatians 4:31

"Alluding to the story of Abraham, Sarah and Hagar, Paul explained the difference between the child of a bondwoman (Hagar) and the child of a freewoman (Sarah). Only the child of the freewoman could enjoy an inheritance; the other was destined to bondage.

Here's the point: each of us – male or female, Jew or Gentile, black or white, rich or poor – can share in God's inheritance. All who trust in Jesus as Saviour become 'not children of the bondwoman but of the free'. We are released from the bondage of the law of God and offered God's grace instead."

ODB

"You are all sons of God through faith in Jesus Christ, for all of you who were baptised into Christ have clothed yourself with Christ. There is neither Jew nor Greek, slave nor free, male nor female, for you are all one in Christ Jesus. If you belong to Christ, then you are Abraham's seed, and heirs according to the promise."

Galations 3:26 – 29

Therefore He is able to save completely those who come to God through Him, because He always lives to intercede for them.

Such a high priest meets our need – one who is holy, blameless, pure, set apart from sinners, exalted above the heavens. Unlike the other high priests, He does not need to offer sacrifices day after day, first for His own sins, and then for the sins of the people. He sacrificed for their sins once

for all when He offered Himself. For the law appoints as
high priests men who are weak; but the oath, which came
after the law, appointed the Son, Who has been made perfect
forever.

Hebrews 7:25 – 28

Keep me safe, O God,
for in You I take refuge.

I said to the Lord, "You are my Lord;
apart from You I have no good thing."
As for the saints who are in the land,
They are the glorious ones in whom is all
my delight.
The sorrows of those will increase
who run after other gods.
I will not pour out their libations of blood
or take up their names on my lips.

Lord, You have assigned me my portion
and my cup;
You have made my lot secure.
The boundary lines have fallen for me in
pleasant places;
surely I have a delightful inheritance.

I will praise the Lord, Who counsels me;
even at night my heart instructs me.
I have set the Lord always before me.

Because He is at my right hand,
I shall not be shaken.

Therefore my heart is glad and my tongue
rejoices;
my body also will rest secure,
because You will not abandon me to the
grave,
nor will you let your Holy One see
decay.
You have made known to me the path of
life;
You will fill me with joy in Your
presence,
with eternal pleasures at Your right hand.

Psalm 16

Then I saw a new heaven and a new earth, for the first heaven
and the first earth had passed away, and there was no longer
any sea. I saw the Holy City, the new Jerusalem, coming out
of heaven from God, prepared as a bride beautifully dressed for
her husband. And I heard a loud voice from the throne saying,
"Now the dwelling of God is with men, and He will live with
them. They will be His people, and God Himself will be with them
and be their God. He will wipe every tear from their eyes. There
will be no more death or mourning or crying or pain, for the old
order of things has passed away.

He who was seated on the throne said, "I am making

everything new!" Then he said, "Write this down, for these words are trustworthy and true."

He said to me: "It is done. I am the Alpha and the Omega, the Beginning and the End. To him who is thirsty I will give to drink without cost from the spring of the water of life. He who overcomes will inherit all this, and I will be his God and he will be my son.

Rev 21:1 – 7

The Lord is my light and my salvation –
Whom shall I fear?
The Lord is the stronghold of my life –
Of whom shall I be afraid?
When evil men advance against me
To devour my flesh,
When my enemies and my foes attack me,
They will stumble and fall.
Though an army besiege me,
My heart will not fear;
Though war break out against me,
Even then will I be confident.

One thing I ask of the Lord,
This is what I seek:
That I may dwell in the house of the Lord
All the days of my life,
To gaze upon the beauty of the Lord

And to seek Him in His temple.
For in the day of trouble
He will keep me safe in His dwelling;
He will hide me in the shelter of His tabernacle
And set me high upon a rock.
Then my head will be exalted
Above the enemies who surround me;
At His tabernacle will I sacrifice with
Shouts of joy;
I will sing and make music to the Lord.

Hear my voice when I call, O Lord;
Be merciful to me and answer me.
My heart says of You "Seek His face!"
Your face, Lord, I will seek.
Do not hide Your face from me,
Do not turn your servant away in anger;
You have been my helper.
Do not reject me or forsake me,
O God my Saviour.
Though my father and mother forsake me,
The Lord will receive me.
Teach me Your way, O Lord;
Lead me in a straight path
Because of my oppressors.
Do not hand me over to the desire of my
Foes,
For false witnesses rise up against me,

Breathing out violence.

I am still confident of this:

I will see the goodness of the Lord

In the land of the living.

Wait for the Lord;

Be strong and take heart

And wait for the Lord.

Psalm 27

For the trumpet will sound, the dead will be raised imperishable,

and we will be changed. For the perishable must clothe itself with

the imperishable, and the mortal with immortality. When the perishable

has been clothed with the imperishable, and the mortal with immortality,

then the saying that is written will come true: Death has been swallowed

up in victory.

Where, O death, is your victory?

Where, O death, is your sting?

1 Corinthians 15:52 – 55

Happiness

I wouldn't presume to say that I have all the answers, after all my idea of happiness may not be others', and apart from this depression is complex and can have many different causes. What I can say is that *my* happiness doesn't exist because I've got no problems. It exists because, although I have many problems, I have found peace.

I am talking from the perspective of someone who has suffered from general depression for many years. It stemmed initially from situations which occurred in my youth which caused unhappiness. Then, as I went into adulthood this unhappiness gained momentum as it was compounded by additional difficulties which I was too young and immature to cope with, in other words issues that went unresolved, and this combination of events caused me to gradually slip into a state of despair. The complex issues that were troubling me became an interwoven jumble in my mind and for many years I was unable even to define what the specific problems were, let alone set about solving them. It was only in 2000 when I set out to find *help* that each different source that I approached helped me to isolate each problem and tackle them one by one. Other people can live a generally happy existence but can be bowled over by a particular event such as the death of a loved one or a loss of employment. Sometimes a combination of events can conspire to pull us into a dark time in our lives, such as a stressful and exhausting period at work combined with taking care of a loved one who is seriously ill. Just as it is very easy to get physically run down and become ill during a time such as this so it is easy to become emotionally run down and depressed. Both cases can usually be very simply diagnosed and treated. It is a good idea to look to others for help and support during times of depression just as you would if you were physically ill, and not try to "go it alone" as I did, but it's best to turn to family members or one or two friends whom you can trust or go to your doctor. One other piece of advice I would offer is to avoid making drastic decisions thinking that a major change will help you get over your depression.

I heard once that life can be a series of peaks and troughs. When we are going through a good spell it's best to be aware that at some point we may be heading for a low spell but similarly if we are experiencing a low time, if we just hang in there, we will eventually begin climbing again. My life has felt like a trough. I gradually slipped downwards until I finally reached the bottom and although reaching the bottom was a totally painful experience, far from killing me, the only outcome was that I started climbing up out the other side. It was only when I had reached rock bottom, and was all done in, that it was possible for God to take me by the hand and begin to pull me up – as the saying goes "human extremity is often the meeting place with God."

Early in my marriage I began attending church, as I had in my youth, as I knew that turning to God would be a good start in solving my problems but answers didn't come all at once as I would have liked them to. Instead, I was given understanding little by little until eventually, twenty years later, God had revealed Himself to me to the extent that I could derive enough peace and comfort from my relationship with Him to enable me to break free from the chains of depression. I cannot place a value on what

I learned over that challenging time, as I read in Our Daily Bread God speaks to us through our circumstances, through other people and by His Spirit through the Scriptures. Over recent years He has spoken to me through Our Daily Bread and through books, poems and songs – many of which I have quoted or quoted from in this book. Looking back, I wouldn't trade my life for another's; our adversities are what shape us (Romans 5:3) and equip us to help and truly empathise with others. Difficult times are the best teachers.

> I have touched the bottom, and it is sound.
> *Joseph Parker*

> Don't let a bleak past cloud a bright future.
> *ODB*

> A rough path is sometimes worth the
> treading if, in so doing, we can
> tread down the brambles in the path
> of another.
> *Anon*

God has different purposes for different people. Some people are delivered from their trials while others are required to go through them so that they can be used to help others, in which case God provides the means and strength to endure.

> Praise be to the God and Father of our Lord Jesus Christ,
> the Father of compassion and the God of all comfort,
> who comforts us in all our troubles, so that we can
> comfort those in any trouble with the comfort we

ourselves have received from God. For just as the sufferings of Christ flow over into our lives, so also through Christ our comfort overflows.

2 Corinthians 1:3 – 5

Those who have suffered are best able to help those who are suffering

ODB

THE BRIDGE BUILDER

An old man going along a highway, came at evening cold and grey;

To a chasm vast and wide and steep, with waters rolling cold and deep.

The old man crossed in the twilight dim, the sullen stream had no fears for him;

But he turned when safe on the other side, and built a bridge to span the tide.

'Old man,' said a fellow pilgrim near,

'You're wasting your strength with building here;

Your journey will end with the ending day, you never again will pass this way.

You've crossed the chasm deep and wide, why build you this bridge at eventide?'

The builder lifted his old grey head, 'Good friend, in the path I have come,' he said,

'There followeth after me today, a youth whose feet must pass this way.

The chasm that was as nought to me, to that fair-haired youth may a pitfall be;

He too must cross in the twilight dim – Good friend,

I'm building this bridge for *him*.'

Will Allen Dromgoole

TREASURES OF DARKNESS

Within the depths of

His darkest clouds

God often seems to bury His

richest treasures –

     silver streaks of growth,

     sterling faith,

     precious gleaming truths –

for His beloved children.

Has a dense cloud of

     doubt,

     pain,

     loss,

     trouble,

     frustration or

     loneliness

Settled over you, dear one?

Search out the treasures of darkness!

The riches of your Heavenly Father, hide there

With your name engraved in silver!

Susan Lenzkes

At age 30 she was ready to give up. She wrote in her diary, "My God, what will become of me? I have no desire but to die." But the dark clouds of despair gave way to the light, and in time she discovered a new purpose for living. When she died at age 90, she had left her mark on history. Some believe that she and those who introduced antiseptics and chloroform to medicine did more than anyone to relieve human suffering in the 19th century. Her name was Florence Nightingale, founder of the nursing profession.

Job went so far as to wish he had never been born (Job 3:1 – 3). But thank God, he didn't end his life. Just as Florence Nightingale came out of her depression and found ways to help others, so too Job lived through his grief, and his experience has become a source of endless comfort to suffering souls.

Maybe you're at the point of not wanting to go on. Being God's child intensifies your desperation, for you wonder how a believer could feel so alone and forsaken. Don't give up. Coming to the end of yourself emotionally could be the most painful experience you've ever encountered. But take courage. Cling to the Lord in faith and start all over. God can use this kind of "beginning from the end."

ODB

Out of the Darkness

Out of the dark forbidding soil,

the pure white lilies grow.

Out of the black and murky clouds,

descends the stainless snow.

Out of the crawling earthbound worm,

a butterfly is born.

Out of the sombre shrouded night,

Behold, a golden morn!
Out of the pain and stress of life,
the peace of God pours down.
Out of the Nails – the Spear- the Cross,
Redemption and a Crown!

Triumph is made from sorrow

I discovered the peace and contentment that comes from patiently waiting while God works His purpose in my life, while moving steadily onward in faith, totally trusting in Him.

Desperately, helplessly, longingly, I cried.

Quietly, patiently, lovingly, God replied.

I pled and I wept for a clue to my fate,

And the Master so gently said, "Child, you must wait!"

"Wait?" you say, "Wait!" my indignant reply.

"Lord, I need answers, I need to know why!

Is Your hand shortened? Or have You not heard?

By faith I have asked, and am claiming Your Word.

"My future, and all to which I can relate

Hangs in the balance, and You tell me to wait?

I am needing a "yes", a go-ahead sign,

Or even a "no" to which I can resign.

"And Lord, You promised, that if we believe,

We need but to ask, and we shall receive.

And Lord, I've been asking, and this is my cry:

I'm weary of asking! I need a reply!"

Then quietly, softly, I learned of my fate

As my Master replied once again, "You must wait."
So, I slumped in my chair, defeated and taut,
And I grumbled to God, "So I'm waiting…for what?"

He seemed then to kneel, and His eyes wept with mine,
And He tenderly said, "I could give you a sign.
I could shake the heavens, and darken the sun.
I could raise the dead and cause mountains to run.
All you seek I could give, and pleased you would be.
You would have what you want – but, you wouldn't know Me.

"You'd not know the depth of My love for each saint,
You'd not know the power that I give to the faint,
You'd not learn to look through the clouds of despair,
You'd not learn to trust just by knowing I'm there,
You'd not know the joy of just resting in Me,
When darkness, and silence were all you could see.

"You'd never experience the fullness of love,
As the peace of My spirit descends like a dove,
You'd know that I give and I save…(for a start),
But you'd not know the depth of the beat of My heart.

"The glow of My comfort late into the night.
The faith that I give when you walk without sight,
The depth that's beyond getting just what you asked,
Of an infinite God, Who makes what you have last.

"You'd never know, should your pain quickly flee,
What it means that "My grace is sufficient for thee".

Yes, your dreams for your loved ones overnight would come true,

But, oh, the loss if I lost what I'm doing in you!

"So, be silent, my child, and in time you will see,

That the greatest of gifts is to get to know Me.

And though oft may My answers seem terribly late,

The wisest of answers is still to "WAIT".

Author Unknown

'Father, Although I Cannot See

Father, although I cannot see

the future You have planned,

And though the path is sometimes dark

and hard to understand;

Yet give me faith, through joy and pain,

to trace Your loving hand.

When I recall that in the past

Your promises have stood

Through each perplexing circumstance

and every changing mood,

I rest content that all things work

together for my good.

Whatever, then, the future brings

of good or seeming ill,

I ask for strength to follow You

and grace to trust You still;

and I would look for no reward,
except to do Your will.

Trust In God

Courage, Brother, do not stumble,
Though your path be dark as night;
There's a star to guide the humble,
Trust in God and do the right.

Let the road be rough and dreary,
And its end far out of sight,
Foot it bravely, strong or weary;
Trust in God and do the right.

Perish policy and cunning,
Perish all that fears the light;
Whether losing, whether winning,
Trust in God and do the right.

Trust no party, sect or faction,
Trust no leaders in the fight;
But in every word and action
Trust in God and do the right.

Simple rule and safest guiding,
Inward peace and inward might,
Star upon our path abiding;
Trust in God and do the right.

Some will hate you, some will love you,

Some will flatter, some will slight;
Cease from man, and look above you,
Trust in God and do the right.

Norman Macleod

Father, I place into Your hands

Father, I place into Your hands
the things that I can't do.
Father, I place into Your hands
the times that I've been through.
Father, I place into Your hands
the way that I should go,
for I know I always can trust You.

Father, I place into Your hands
my friends and family.
Father, I place into Your hands
the things that trouble me.
Father, I place into Your hands
the person I would be,
for I know I always can trust You.

Be patient, then, brothers, until the Lord's coming. See how the farmer waits for the land to yield its valuable crop and how patient he is for the autumn and spring rains. You too, be patient and stand firm, because the Lord's coming is near.
James 5:7 & 8

People pursue happiness because they feel that it is what life is all about, their purpose in life. After all, the other end of the spectrum to happiness is unhappiness. But we weren't put on this earth primarily to be *happy*. Christ's ultimate purpose in living a human life was to suffer and die for us. In 1 Peter 4:12 &13 we are told that we can expect to suffer also. "Dear friends, do not be surprised at the painful trial you are suffering...but rejoice that you participate in the sufferings of Christ, so that you may be overjoyed when His glory is revealed." The apostle Paul talks about this also. In Philippians 1:29 he says "For it has been granted to you on behalf of Christ not only to believe in Him, but also to suffer for Him." Paul himself suffered floggings, humiliation and imprisonment, he knew what it was like to be in need and to go hungry but he was able to bear his suffering and conclude, "I have learned to be content whatever the circumstances" (Philippians 4:11) because he knew what God ultimately had in store for him – "I have fought the good fight, I have finished the race, I have kept the faith. Now there is in store for me the crown of righteousness, which the Lord, the righteous Judge will award me on that day – and not only to me, but also to all who have longed for His appearing."

Struggle is one evidence of God's work in our lives.

ODB

Happiness is not the only thing in life worth aspiring to.

Denyse Devlin

Shall we accept good from God, and not trouble?

Job 2:10

**We don't complain when we receive blessings
so why complain at adversity?**

In his book 'If This Is a Man' by Primo Levi written in 1947, about an Italian Jew, a Chemist and Holocaust survivor from Turin in Northern Italy, who survived Auschwitz concentration camp by maintaining a positive spirit against all odds, he stated that hopelessness and despair were as great a killer in the camps as starvation and freezing conditions. He was so determined to be positive that he was able to experience happiness even though it was fleeting and momentary, but it was enough to keep his spirit alive.

We can have hope if we believe in God's promises for our future and because the Holy Spirit is always with us. We can believe and have faith in God's promises because we can see the evidence of God's work in our lives, the way He has helped us through our struggles and by His many blessings. "He who has begun a good work in you will perform it until the Day of Jesus Christ" Philippians 1:6. We also know that Christ, Who came to live amongst us and Who understands us, intercedes constantly on our behalf with His Father. God also promises that He will never allow us to be tempted beyond what we are able (1 Corinthians 10:13). When you are tempted He will also provide a way out so that you can endure it.

We have one who speaks to the Father in our defence – Jesus Christ, the Righteous One.

1 John 2:1

For this God is our God for ever and ever; He will be our guide even to the end.

Psalms 48:14

But those who hope in the Lord will renew their strength. They will soar on wings like eagles; they will run and not grow weary, they will walk and not be faint.

Isaiah 40:31

If I am looking at life through a perspective of gratitude and hope….I will live and think differently than if my view was one of bitterness and anger. A true perspective helps me keep my priorities straight. The big things in my life – my family, my work, my faith in God – stay big, and receive most of my energy. The little things receive less attention. I am able to laugh at myself and my problems, to find contentment in my present circumstances, and to maintain hope for the future.

Thomas Kinkade

When we have hope, we discover powers within ourselves we may have never known – the power to make sacrifices, to endure, to heal, and to love.

Christopher Reeve

Praise be to the God and Father of our Lord Jesus Christ! In His great mercy He has given us new birth into a living hope through the resurrection of Jesus Christ from the dead, and into an inheritance that can never perish, spoil or fade – kept in heaven for you, who through faith are shielded by God's power until the coming of the salvation that is ready to be revealed in the last time. In this you greatly rejoice, though now for a little while you may have had to suffer grief in all kinds of trials. These have come so that your faith – of greater worth than gold, which perishes even though refined by fire – may be proved genuine and may result in praise, glory and honour when Jesus Christ is revealed. Though you have not seen Him, you love Him; and even though you do not see Him now, you believe in Him and are filled with an inexpressible and glorious joy, for you are receiving the goal of your faith, the salvation of your souls.

1 Peter 1:3 – 9

Brothers, as an example of patience in the face of suffering, take the prophets who spoke in the name of the Lord. As you know, we consider blessed those who have persevered. You have heard of Job's   perseverance and have seen what the Lord finally brought about. The Lord is full of compassion and mercy.

James 5:10 & 11

The Lord is full of compassion and mercy and...

Humble yourselves, therefore, under God's mighty hand, that He may lift you up in due time. Cast all your anxiety on Him because He cares for you.

1 Peter 5:6 & 7

...He cares for you

God "is near to those that are broken at heart"

Psalms 34:18

He is the one "who comforts the depressed."

2 Corinthians 7:6

New American Standard Bible

Peace I leave with you; My peace I give you. I do not give to you as the world gives. Do not let your hearts be troubled and do not be afraid.

John 14:27

Don't be afraid

Only when we are no longer afraid do we begin to live.
Dorothy Thompson
The Christian finds safety not in the absence of danger
but in the presence of God.
Anon

The name of the Lord is a strong tower;
the righteous run to it and are safe.
Proverbs 18:10

Worry does not empty tomorrow of its sorrow,
it empties today of its strength.
Corrie Ten Boom

Don't worry

In You the fatherless find compassion.
Hosea 14:3

"For I know the plans I have for you," declares the Lord,
"plans to prosper

you and not to harm you, plans to give you hope and a future."
Jeremiah 29:11

In times of suffering, it's important to consider what God
would have us teach, as well as what He would have us learn.
ODB

Our difficulties can bring out qualities in us which may not show themselves ordinarily; others see the power of God working through our weakness.

Don't let life happen to you. Let life happen through you.

ODB

Allow God to work through you. Don't look at life as something coming at you and therefore shield yourself from life's trials, let God's life and love be channelled through you, blessing you on its way to blessing others.

<u>The cycle of Faith and Doubt</u>

All areas of life have their cycles. A vocation, a marriage, and a relationship with Jesus generally begin with a honeymoon period, then enter a time during which the realities of life gradually replace the early building stage. This often leads into a time marked by varying degrees of disillusionment and discontent.

It is at this point that crucial decisions must be made. At work, one can quit, continue as a disgruntled worker, or see the problems through. In marriage, one can escape by divorce, continue in a lacklustre relationship, or set about to mend the marriage. In the Christian life, one can drop out, continue as an unhappy and defeated believer, or determine to work through the difficulties.

Going the full cycle often brings on a new level of satisfaction in the workplace, lifts honeymoon love to the level of mature mutually-enriching love, and transforms the euphoric faith in which we began into confident trust. Even then, struggles will continue.

As long as we are imperfect people living in this fallen world, we will confront doubts. But Jesus promised, "I am the light of the world. He who follows Me shall not walk in darkness, but have the light of life" (John 8:12). Because of our human frailty, we will sometimes step off His path into the darkness. But if we follow the hymnwriter's admonition to trust and obey, we will soon be back on His path. The light of Christ, not the darkness will be our home.

Why Christians Doubt
RBC Discovery Series

You are all sons of the light and sons of the day.
We do not belong to the night or to the darkness.
1 Thessalonians 5:5

We are God's "fellow workers" (1 Cor 3:9). When the Israelites arrived at Kadesh, in the desert of Zin, there was no water. In Numbers 20:11, at God's command, Moses struck a rock and water gushed out to provide water for the thirsty Israelites and their livestock. Moses struck the rock – an action that could have been done by you or me or anyone, God provided the water – from the depths of the earth. The two worked together. All we need to do is obey, God will do the rest.

Let us then approach the throne of grace with confidence, so that we may receive mercy and find grace to help us in our time of need.
Hebrews 4:16

I've learned that happiness has very little to do with feelings and emotions. I've found that feelings are flighty, fickle, unstable, temporary and are not to be trusted whereas true happiness comes from things that are solid such as the wisdom, knowledge, understanding and discernment.

During the difficult times in our marriage, on a couple of occasions I developed feelings for someone else, they were kindly individuals and I felt a connection with them. Although I had no control over my feelings and emotions, I did have control over how I *acted* on them by depending on God's word and principles to guide me. If I had given in to my feelings I would have caused my husband a great deal of pain and heartache, possibly even creating an irreparable situation. In addition to this, I knew that I didn't have the right to be happy at the expense of *his* happiness.

Apply your heart to instruction

and your ears to words of knowledge

Proverbs 23:12

Trust in the Lord with all your heart and lean

not on your own understanding.

Proverbs 3:5

I urge you to abstain from sinful desires, which war against

your soul.

1 Peter 2:11

An attitude of joy is not based on what we *feel* but on

what we *know* of God and His work in our lives.

ODB

I have learned that worship and happiness are directly related and that worship is not confined to a certain place or day of the week. Every thought and action can be an act of worship. I worship God by being thankful for all that He blesses me with and an appreciative attitude leads to happiness; if we are truly thankful about something it *becomes* a blessing. I worship God by the way I conduct myself and by the way I treat others. This has helped me to become a better person and has resulted in my having happier relationships with other people. I worship God by doing my best at whatever I turn my hand to and because I strive for God's recognition alone and try not to place importance on recognition from those around me, I never have to feel that my hard work and effort goes unnoticed and unappreciated. I can always feel encouraged that God sees all that I do and is pleased with me.

When I worship God I also fulfil His command to obey Him because it is not possible to disobey and worship at the same time, worship is the antithesis of sin. When my sin is not distancing me from God I can be sure that He is with me, and knowing that God is constantly with me is essential to my happiness.

God has promised those who worship and obey Him a wonderful future in fellowship with Him. My happiness lies therefore in hope and confidence that everything will work to my good despite the trials I may experience in this life. The suffering and hardship that I have experienced already has changed me for the better, and I know that it is being used to perfect God's work in me.

Because I am in constant communion with God I am always receptive to His blessings, He answers my prayers and the evidence of His help all through the day in countless ways gives me a quiet but powerful sense of joy and encouragement. One way He manifests Himself to us is through His creation and I feel that He showers me with, what I call, little gifts of grace throughout the day which I would miss if I wasn't receptive to Him. If I didn't look often to the sky I would miss the many beautiful sunrises, sunsets and spectacular cloud formations, the sight of which I find intensely moving.

This is love for God: to obey His commands.

1 John 5:3

And we know that in all things God works for the good
of those who love Him, who have been called according to
His purpose.

Romans 8:28

I have learned that knowing that there is a purpose to life is, in itself, wonderful. It is the sort of knowledge that brings much hope and encouragement and makes it possible to cope with daily problems and setbacks. Knowing that I am living a useful life is deeply satisfying. I won't deny that having a steady income and no debt has brought ease to our lives, but on the other hand I have never bought or possessed anything that has brought me as much happiness as the joy of answered prayer; the joy of knowing that, through the *power* of prayer, I can take care of all those who are dear to me whether they be near or far; the joy of knowing that one day I will see all the loved ones that I have lost; the joy of getting up at the crack of dawn, while the rest of the household sleeps, and drawing close to God through the pages of my Bible; the joy of singing in church in the company of all my dear friends; the joy of seeing how my children have flourished because our home is no longer full of sadness and acrimony, but rather peace and happiness; the joy of sitting back in a pub and quietly observing my elderly friends as they tuck into a good meal and enjoy the opportunity of being able to meet together; the joy of watching the flowers in my garden flourish under my amateur care and sitting quietly, curled up in my favourite armchair with a cup of tea in my hand, watching the birds flutter around the bird feeder and splashing in the bird bath.

For the secret of man's being is not only to live but to have
something to live for.

Dostoyevsky

You may give without loving but you can't love without giving.
ODB

If I give all I possess to the poor...but have not love, I gain nothing
1 Corinthians 13:3

Your beauty should not come from outward adornment, such as braided hair and the wearing of gold jewellery and fine clothes. Instead, it should be that of your inner self, the unfading beauty of a gentle and quiet spirit, which is of great worth in God's sight. For this is the way of the holy women of the past who put their hope in God used to make themselves beautiful.
1 Peter 3:3 - 5

Man cannot find happiness when he lives only for himself.
ODB

But as for me, it is good to be near to God.
Psalm 73:28

Let me hold lightly things of this earth;

Transient treasures, what are they worth?

Moths can corrupt them, rust can decay;

All their bright beauty fades in a day.
Nicholson

The temporary nature of material wealth makes it a poor bargain in the search for security in an insecure world
ODB

I have learned that life is about relationships and for better or for worse we need other people – we cannot 'go it alone.' The most miserable time I have ever experienced in my life was the period during my depression when I tried to get by on my own. Without other people in my life I became completely self-absorbed, my mind was devoid of all thoughts apart from those about myself and my problems which only served to perpetuate my depression. When I got to know other people I gained much encouragement from the realisation that I had a lot in common with many of them who had experienced similar things to what I had, and even further encouragement from discovering that I could use my experiences to help others. I began to realise that God designed us so that we need other people and that it is through our relationships with others that we learn how to love. Love is the central theme of the Bible, "And now these three remain: faith, hope and love. But the greatest of these is love," (1 Corinthians 13:13) as love leads to obedience and obedience is the path to the everlasting life that God wants us to share with Him.

I learned the value of Christian relationships in helping me to stay close to God. When we spend time with other Christians they help us to keep focused on what is important. Christianity is a very narrow path and as soon as we become detached from the fellowship of others of a like mind it is very easy to fall prey to subtle worldly influences. More often than not the first thing to suffer is our lifeline to God – our prayer life.

Often when I had a problem I would try to work my way through it on my own but after, I thought, looking at all the angles I would quite often come to a negative conclusion which would on many occasions lead me to despair. This was always followed by my cutting myself off from other people. One particular friend of mine would contact me after not hearing from me for a while and she would end up meeting with me and we would talk the problem over. After we had gone our separate ways I would mull over what she had said and I would always find something to hold on to, something that would help me to keep on going. We never have all the answers, we need counsel and input from others to be able to make informed decisions. "Without counsel plans fail, but with many advisers they succeed" (Proverbs 15:22). We can end up in a lot of trouble when we listen to our own advice.

I began to look forward to going to church where I knew the service as a whole would be uplifting and encouraging - the worship and the message – and I looked forward to congregating with people where I could find, as well as give, support and encouragement that would help me during the course of the following week until it was time to meet again.

My enjoyment of going to church increased when I began to get involved in different activities and events. I began to see that, just like everyone else in the congregation, I had been blessed with specific skills which I could use to contribute to the services as well as the outreach activities. I began to feel valued as a member of that congregation in as much as I knew that if I didn't attend for any reason people would be sure to ask after me.

A while after my husband and I set out to work on our marriage relationship I came to realise that love is not an emotion it is a choice. I consciously set out to downplay my husband's faults and focus on his qualities, I began to pray for him, not that God would change him but for help in all aspects in his life and when he hurt me I found comfort in talking to God about it and at least attempting to hand the hurt over to Him. It's not an easy habit to get into, nothing worthwhile comes easily, but it is a way of handling problems that has proved itself to be far more successful than anything I've tried in the past.

We once had a discussion about arranged marriages because I felt sure that many of them must be successful. We came to the conclusion that kindness and gentleness must be the key. We agreed that even if the individuals involved didn't find each other attractive at first, that in time kindness would win them over and make them appealing to each other. We felt that it would be impossible to resist someone who is consistently kind because kindness is love. Love is not feelings, it is a doing word, it is the action of genuine kindness. I emphasise *genuine* because there are two types of kindness, one is selfless and genuine and the other is self-serving where individuals perform acts of kindness in order to become popular with people.

The loss that I have experienced in my life has taught me not to take other people for granted and that it is important to show people how much you love and value them by how you treat them. I've also learned that it's important to tell people you love them while you have the chance. Even though my Mum and I didn't get on, when my son was born and I experienced all that was involved in looking after a baby even down to keeping them clean and comfortable, I wrote to my mum and thanked her for the way she took care of me because I know I was well looked after. I also made a point of writing to my grandparents to tell them how much I loved them and to let them know what they meant to me. They received this letter shortly before my Grandmother passed away. I even wrote to my husband's Gran until she died so that, looking back, he would never have any regrets because men are not always good at keeping in touch.

Without relationships with others we could never learn how to love God. A person's inability to have a close relationship with God, which sometimes manifests itself in a difficulty in approaching God in prayer can, in some cases, be traced back to a poor relationship with the individual's father, especially if the father has been particularly strict or overbearing.

I once viewed God as being an authority in my life; someone who is good to me and whom I can trust. Because of this I felt that I wanted to please Him although I couldn't say that I loved Him, any more than I could love a kind employer. It was only when I started reading my Bible in depth that I can honestly say that I began to love God, somehow reading God's words and getting to know Him intimately through the Bible made my relationship with Him far more personal. Just as reading about the works of Mother Theresa and the Sisters of Charity inspired me to want to emulate them so reading about God's works inspired me to want to emulate Him. We are told that as the Holy Spirit works within us and the fruits of the Holy Spirit begin to manifest themselves in us we grow to be more like God (Galatians 5:22-23).

Just as the lowest part of my life coincided with not attending church, reading the Bible or praying so the joy that I experience now comes from doing all three. My affiliation with a church where I receive support and encouragement and where I find acceptance and my drawing close to God through His word and through prayer has brought me the joy and contentment that God promised it would.

And this is love: that we walk in obedience to His commands. As you have heard from the beginning, His command is that you walk in love.

2 John 6

Dear friends, let us love one another, for love comes from God. Everyone who loves has been born of God and knows God... since God so loved us, we also ought to love one another. No-one has ever seen God; but if we love one another, God lives in us and His love is made complete in us.

1 John 4:7 – 8; 11 – 12

LOVE

Love can change

the attitude

Love can change the mind

Love can make us likeable

Love can make us kind.

Love can break the barriers

Love can set us free

In other words –

Love can mould a new life

For you and me.

Otis Skilling

This is from a little plaque that stands in my bedroom

The happiness of your life depends on the quality of your thoughts.

You have power over your mind – not outside events.

Your life is what your thoughts make it.

ODB

As [a person] thinks in his heart, so is he.

Proverbs 23:7

When Christ comes to live in us we are changed. We are no longer just ordinary people but we become the dwelling place of the Holy Spirit.

ODB

My religion is Kindness.
Dalai Lama

Now to each one the manifestation of the Spirit is given for the common good.
1 Corinthians 12:7

The Holy Spirit gives every follower of Christ at least one spiritual gift. These God-given abilities are bestowed so that the church can function effectively and grow strong.

Blest Be the Tie that Binds

Blest be the tie that binds our hearts in Christian love;

The fellowship of kindred minds is like to that above.

Before our Father's throne we pour our ardent prayers;

Our fears, our hopes, our aims are one, our comforts and our cares.

We share our mutual woes, our mutual burdens bear;

And often for each other flows the sympathising tear.

When we asunder part, it gives us inward pain;

But we shall still be joined in heart, and hope to meet again.

Text: John Fawcett

Music: Hans G. Naegeli

Satan wants to defeat us with heavy burdens, but fellow believers by their love and support can minimise the suffering he causes.

ODB

The Sovereign LORD has given

me a well-instructed tongue,

to know the word that sustains

the weary. He wakens me morning

by morning, wakens my ear to listen

like one being instructed.

Isaiah 50:4

God doesn't comfort us to make us comfortable, but to make us comforters.

2 Corinthians 1:4

Make sure nobody pays back wrong for wrong, but always try to be kind to each other and to everyone else. Be joyful always; pray continually; give thanks in all circumstances, for this is God's will for you in Christ Jesus.

1 Thessalonians 5:15 – 18

Negative thoughts or actions never result in a positive outcome

Do not say "I'll pay you back for this wrong!"
Wait for the Lord, and He will deliver you.
Proverbs 20:22

When tempted to fight fire with fire, remember
that the Fire Department usually uses water.

Anon

SING as though no one can hear you

DANCE as though no one is watching you

LOVE as though you have never been hurt

If we allow past hurt to diminish our ability to love we lose something in ourselves.

If we hand our hurt over to God we will always have the courage to love wholeheartedly and experience the joy that love brings

Do What You Can to Help Yourself

There were times when this world seemed a very hard and callous place to me, but as angry as it made me to have to accept it, no-one was going to wave a magic wand and make all my problems disappear. Life wasn't going to come to a standstill just because I was struggling to cope, everything would go on as usual, day after day. After all, over the years on the news, I had witnessed scenes of people in third world countries dying from malnutrition and nothing miraculous was occurring to help *them*. The world owed me nothing - it seemed to me that I needed to do what I could to help myself. There were many things that either I couldn't change or else I didn't know how to, but there were some things that I could. For instance, how could I go around feeling miserable about being overweight if I wasn't ready to go on a diet or exercise?

Once I felt that I could approach God once more I set up my old routine of daily prayer. It suits me best to do so early in the day as it gives me the means to be able to begin the day feeling confident. Also, I find that once I get embroiled in my daily activities it is so easy for prayer to go out the window. Well actually I pray and talk to God all day and every day because I look to Him to help me with every aspect of my day from moment to moment. I, personally, like to pray in the car as I drive home from dropping my daughter at college. The route that I take is so beautiful through the English countryside and it makes my spirits soar – I feel like God is all around me and I feel inspired to pray.

My prayer always begins with thanking my Father for all that He gives to me and blesses me with – my family and friends, my home with all its appliances, gas, electricity and hot and cold running water, our cars, our jobs, our health, my clothes, for the fact that I know what my purpose is in life, for the fact that my life *has* a purpose. I also thank God for being who He is and for the fact that He has promised me eternal life in His presence. After I've reeled off all I have to be grateful for I feel a new appreciation for each and every thing all over again and this, in turn, lifts my spirits – thankfulness always leads to joy.

I always pray that God will find my prayer acceptable to Him because I never want God to think that I'm being casual in the way I address Him and yet I talk to Him with ease as if He were a friend Whom I am conversing with. I want Him to know that I respect His authority as our Creator and yet, at the same time, that I am so glad that He has made it possible for me to call on Him at any time, day or night.

I ask my Father to take care of all of those whom I care about and all of those whom He has put in my path to intercede for and although I mention names of specific people on my mind I know that God will remember all those whom I have committed to Him in prayer over the years, He remembers them all by name and He will look after them for me every day. I pray for anyone and everyone. If I pass an elderly couple in the street I commit them to God's care, if I see an ambulance I pray, if I see a lonely looking youth wandering along the road I pray. Knowing that I can take care of people all over the world - whether they be family, friends or strangers – by committing them into God's care through prayer is an inexhaustible source of joy to me. It means that when I think of family and friends whom I have left behind because of leaving the country or who themselves have moved to different parts of the world, I never have to feel helpless to be able to take care of them still.

As I drive through the council estate where I live I pray for my community and that God will put people in my path whom I can help and bring to Him. I ask Him especially to please look after 'my old ladies' as I affectionately refer to the elderly ladies who I chauffeur to different events.

I ask that God's Kingdom will come just as soon as possible to end all evil, suffering and heartache in the world. Then I ask for Him to fill me with the strength that I need to get through that day, only ever asking for strength for one day at a time and never being concerned about that which I will need for tomorrow. And I ask God to help me and my family to put in a good day's work and to do our best for that day.

Once I've finished praying I set off feeling confident that I will be given the strength that I need to get through the day no matter what it may bring and I know that everyone whom I care about is being looked after for another day.

The prayer of a righteous man is powerful and effective.
James 5:16

We can find help from many sources – friends, counsellors, books – but there's nothing better than the support and strength we get from God when we pray.

ODB

At one time or another, during times of personal struggle or loss, we've all heard people tell us they would "pray for us." Just an expression, I'd always thought, until I felt the power of that sentiment when it is offered, and *meant*, by tens of thousands of people. The feeling is overwhelming; I have no doubt that being on the receiving end of so much spiritual energy has gone a long way to sustain me over the last couple of years. I no longer underestimate the power of prayer.

Michael J. Fox

An observation from someone who has benefitted from the prayers of others - Michael J. Fox has suffered from Parkinson's disease since 1991. I know how I feel when others pray for me.

PRAYING

Lord of my days

I have so often said, 'Teach me to pray'.

As a child I learned the prayer of prayers,

The Lord's Prayer.

I committed to memory

The great traditional prayers of the church.

They have been a foundation

And support for all my prayers.

But there are times when words fail me,

When all the prayers I've ever heard or read

Seem inappropriate,

And the jumble of thoughts,

Worries, questions,

Rushing through my head

Reduce me to silence,

Or the single plea,

'Lord, help me.'

Time has taught me
That I can pray without words.
You, Who number the hairs on my head,
Know my every thought.
You know the decisions I must make,
Every problem, every failure,
Every triumph, every joy
Is known to you.
And it is enough to close my eyes,
To come into Your presence and say,
'Lord, You know what is happening to me,
In my work, in my marriage,
In my mind and in my body.
Loving Lord, help me.'

Sometimes I have felt guilty
That I have not expressed my gratitude
For the love I have received.
But now I know
That I do not need to find acceptable words.
I need only be aware of You.
I see now that when music moves me to tears
It is because I have perceived Your presence in the
 melody.
When, in a moment of drama,
Or at the peak of an artist's performance,
I feel a shiver running down my spine,

It is because Your Spirit is passing through me.

A peal of warm-hearted laughter
Is a response to Your love
Living in people,
And now at last I dimly see
That prayer is not only words
But a way of living,
An awareness of Your presence,
A perception of the power of Your Spirit in my life;
Supporting me,
Healing me,
Loving me.
Lord
Teach me to pray
With my life.

Frank Topping

In 2000 I started reading a daily devotional, the particular one I read is Our Daily Bread which is produced by RBC Ministries (Radio Bible Class). Ever since then I have made a point of reading as soon as I get up in the morning and it has been a wonderful source of encouragement to me with its daily scripture and commentary. When I woke up day after day feeling low or after a night of bad dreams it would comfort me and get me focused on something positive to begin the day. What I've found so incredible, too, is that if I had something on my mind, if something was troubling me or if I had a question that needed answering, the reading for that particular day would always provide me with an answer – it was as though it had been written just for me. Other people whom I have spoken to about it have had similar experiences.

The commentaries are full of interesting facts which have really helped increase my general knowledge.

Reading through my Bible from start to finish has been an absolute joy to me – it has completely opened up the Bible and it has come alive for me, for one thing it has helped me to understand how God sees us. When I read His life-giving book I feel like I am in conversation with someone who is telling me all about Himself – as I listen I get to know who He is and how His mind works. The more I get to know Him - as I see His great love for humanity being revealed, His fairness in dealing with situations, His mercy and His compassion - the more I love Him and want to be like Him, He makes me want to be a better person.

There is something about reading God's word that conveys the essence of Him in a way that nothing else can, it is truly a remarkable experience and one that leaves me feeling uplifted every time I do.

And we, who with unveiled faces all reflect the Lord's glory, are being transformed into His likeness with ever-increasing glory, which comes from the Lord, who is the Spirit.
2 Corinthians 3:18

All scripture is God-breathed and is useful for teaching, rebuking, correcting and training in righteousness, so that the man of God may be thoroughly equipped for every good work.
2 Timothy 3:16 & 17

O Lord, our Lord,
how majestic is Your name in all the
earth!
You have set Your glory

above the heavens,
From the lips of children and infants
    You have ordained praise
because of Your enemies,
    to silence the foe and the avenger.

When I consider Your heavens,
    the work of Your fingers,
the moon and the stars,
    which You have set in place,
what is man that You are mindful of him,
    the son of man that You care for him?
You made him a little lower than the
        Heavenly beings
    and crowned him with glory and
        honour.

You made him ruler over the works of
        Your hands;
You put everything under his feet:
    all flocks and herds,
and the beasts of the field,
    the birds of the air,
    and the fish of the sea,
    all that swim the paths of the seas.
O Lord, our Lord,
    how majestic is Your name in all the
        earth!

Psalm 8

I love to sing, and with so many beautiful songs and hymns around (traditional and contemporary) what more enjoyable way to worship is there? What greater outlet for joy? It's been my experience that when God senses in me a spirit of *genuine* and *meaningful* worship and thanksgiving, *whether in good times or bad*, He imparts through the songs that I'm singing His spirit of encouragement, empowerment and healing.

The Heart of Worship

When the music fades all is stripped away,
And I simply come,
Longing just to bring something that's of worth,
That will bless Your heart.

I'll bring you more than a song,
For a song in itself,
Is not what you have required.
You search much deeper within,
Through the way things appear.
You're looking into my heart.

I'm coming back to the heart of worship,
And it's all about You,
All about You, Jesus.

I'm sorry Lord for the thing I've made it,
When it's all about You,
All about You, Jesus.

King of endless worth no one could express,
How much You deserve.
Though I'm weak and poor all I have is Yours,
Every single breath.

Matt Redman

You Are My Anchor

You are my anchor,
My light and my salvation.
You are my refuge,
My heart will not fear.
Though my foes surround me
On every hand,
They will stumble and fall
While in grace I stand.
In my day of trouble
You hide me and set me above
To sing this song of love.

One thing I will ask of You, this will I pray:
To dwell in Your house, O Lord, every day,
To gaze upon Your lovely face
And rest in the Father's embrace.

Teach me Your way, Lord,
Make straight the path before me.
Do not forsake me, my hope is in You.
As I walk through life, I am confident

I will see Your goodness with every step,
And my heart directs me to seek You
In all that I do,
So I will wait for You.

Stuart Townend

This song fills me with joy and the confidence to be able to handle anything that comes my way.

The Voice of Hope

As high as the heavens are above the earth
So high are Your ways to mine
Ways so perfect they never fail me
I know You are good all the time

And through the storm
Yet I will praise You
Despite it all
Yet I will sing
Through good or bad
Yet I will worship
For You remain the same
King of kings

You are the voice of hope
The anchor of my soul
Where there seems to be no way
You make it possible
You are the Prince of Peace

Amidst adversity
My lips will shout for joy
To You the Most High

You were the One before time began
There's nothing beyond Your control
My confidence my assurance
Rest in Your unchanging Word

Lara Martin

Be 'unwaveringly steadfast' (scripture)

Jesus Be The Centre

Jesus, be the Centre,
Be my source, be my light,
Jesus.

Jesus, be the Centre,
Be my hope, be my song,
Jesus.

Be the fire in my heart,
Be the wind in these sails,
Be the reason that I live,
Jesus, Jesus.

Jesus, be my vision,
Be my path, be my guide,
Jesus.

Michael Frye

I think of Jesus as being the centre of my existence and the soul motivation in my life – my driving force, as is 'the wind in these sails' to a ship.

In Christ Alone

In Christ alone, my hope is found,
He is my light, my strength, my song,
This cornerstone, this solid Ground,
Firm through the fiercest drought and storm.
What heights of love, what depths of peace,
When fears are stilled, when strivings cease,
My comforter, my All in All,
Here in the love of Christ I stand.

In Christ alone – Who took on flesh,
Fullness of God in helpless babe.
This gift of love and righteousness,
Scorned by the ones He came to save.
Till on that cross as Jesus died,
The wrath of God was satisfied,
For every sin on Him was laid.
Here in the death of Christ I live.

There in the ground His body lay,
Light of the world by darkness slain.
Then bursting forth in glorious Day,
Up from the grave He rose again.
And as He stands in victory,
Sin's curse has lost its grip on me.

For I am His and He is mine,
Bought by the precious blood of Christ.

No guilt in life, no fear in death,
This is the power of Christ in me.
From life's first cry, to final breath,
Jesus commands my destiny.
No power of hell, no scheme of man,
Can ever pluck me from His hand,
Till He returns or calls me home,
Here in the power of Christ I'll stand.
Stuart Townend & Keith Getty

I give them eternal life, and they shall never perish; no-one can snatch them out of My hand. My Father, Who has given them to Me, is greater than all; no-one can snatch them out of My Father's hand. I and the Father are one.
John 10:28 – 30

Throughout his life, my dad has set a good example by taking regular exercise and when my children were little I began doing, what I found to be, very effective muscle toning exercises called Callanetics. I did try jogging once or twice. I've seen so many people, in my life, jogging along in a leisurely fashion looking very cool and perspiring politely into their sweatbands – not I! I have pounded the streets, sweating profusely, gasping and wheezing, my face distorted with effort and as red as a beetroot – and that was going downhill! Not a pretty sight. My exercise routine was disrupted by our move to England but in 2000 I resumed it and have kept it up to this day. I haven't succeeded in losing much weight but I feel so much better for it. I only do about twenty minutes a day but as soon as I don't exercise for a couple of days I start feeling uncomfortable. I've managed to shrug off the sluggish feeling that used to accompany lack of activity and once I've exercised, bathed, dressed and put on a little make up I feel energised, confident and ready for the day. I discipline myself to get up and exercise every day, I don't need any gadgets so I have no excuse for not exercising – I can't use the excuse that I didn't have time to get to the gym. There were days, during the time in my life when it was difficult to get up in the mornings, when I forced myself to get on with it. I disciplined myself to get up each cold and dark morning in winter. On a couple of occasions, I sat and cried because I just didn't want to do it, I didn't want to move let alone exercise, but I made myself do it and once I did I always felt so much better. I knew if I didn't exercise I would feel worse, it would lower my confidence, lessen my energy and my day would get off to a bad start. Now I am in such a routine it is second nature to get up and exercise every day – I don't even have to think about it. I have the television on while I am exercising and I put it on the Breakfast show so that I can watch the news and the weather report, but as well as this quite a lot of banter goes on between the TV presenters and quite often something amusing is said that tickles my funny bone. If you can picture the scene: it's six o'clock in the morning and in wintertime it is still pitch black outside at this time, the rest of the household is still fast asleep and there am I lying on my back on the lounge carpet giggling in the process of trying to do my sit ups.

DISCIPLINE

Doing what we don't want to do to achieve what we've always wanted.

I've found that if you conquer discipline in one aspect of your life it becomes easier to do so in other aspects of your life also

To look at the funny side of things is a good habit to get into. I read once that no-one is unhappy every minute of every day and I'm sure that except for extreme cases where people are suffering in diabolical situations this is true. I taught myself to make the most of enjoyable moments such as watching a funny film or enjoying a delicious meal or enjoying the company of a good friend. One of the most valuable things I've learned in life is how to laugh at myself - not take myself too seriously.

A cheerful heart is good medicine,
but a crushed spirit dries up the bones.
Proverbs 17:22

Sometimes your joy is the source of your smile –
and sometimes your smile is the source of your joy.
Thich Nhat Hanh

A smile on the outside can cheer you up on the inside

I ask God to help me through the day, moment by moment. The more I talk to God the closer to Him I feel. James 4:8 says "Come near to God and He will come near to you." The closer to God I feel the more confident I am. I wouldn't ever want to do anything to distance myself from Him – that's something I'd never want to go through again. I am terrified at the thought of ever sliding back into depression and this causes me to keep a tight control of my thoughts and what is influencing my thoughts. I make a conscious effort to avoid all negative influences and rather absorb positive ones. I am careful of the company I keep, the music I listen to, what I watch on TV and what I read. When I go to the library I ask God to help me find books that will be uplifting. I am blessed to have an absolute joy of learning and I love to watch informative programmes and read books and watch films that are interesting and inspirational. I also enjoy nothing more than to listen to people who are knowledgeable and who inspire me.

Every morning I get up early to follow my positive routine of prayer, reading 'Our Daily Bread' and reading my Bible, followed by exercising, bathing, dressing and applying a little make-up. I have been doing this for a number of years now and find that it is the best way to begin a successful day. During my days of depression I would try as far as possible to get up, get dressed and put on some make-up as I found that if I looked good then I felt better (though the end result did not *always* make me look good as one day I was getting ready for work and applying my make-up in the gloom of early morning light as I didn't want to put on the bedroom light and wake up my husband. Later on that morning I happened to catch a glimpse of myself in the mirror in the ladies' loo at work and saw that I'd overdone the face powder and my face had a bright orange glow – very similar to a pumpkin). It was a simple way that I could help myself, even though at the time it was sometimes the hardest thing to do.

I believe that there were certain requirements for healing that God expected of me: to accept and obey His will in my life, to look to Him prayerfully for all my daily needs, to look to Him prayerfully for healing, to wait patiently for healing and, while I was waiting, to move forward in faith doing what I could to help myself.

For each one should carry his own load.

Galatians 6:5

In all your ways acknowledge Him, and He will make your *paths straight. Proverbs 3:6*

Success comes in a very prickly package and whether you choose to accept it or not is up to you. Surround yourself with people who challenge you and who are smarter than you. Always be the student.

Sandra Bullock

The happiest people are those who think the most interesting thoughts. Those who decide to use leisure as a means of mental development, who love good music, good books, good pictures, good company, good conversation, are the happiest people in the world. And they are not only happy in themselves, they are the cause of happiness in others.

William Lyon Phelps, Educator and Literary Critic

We must have courage, faith… and chocolate fudge cake

This is from my favourite mug - every morning when I have my breakfast I make a point of drinking my tea out of a mug that has been given to me by a loved one. Along with a positive routine of prayer, Bible study and exercise it's a great way to start the day.

I Am a New Creation

Who is this person who climbs out of bed every morning, come rain or shine praising God and thankful for another day? Who is this person who falls into bed at night praising God and looking forward to the next? Who is this person with clear eyes and a joyful heart? Who is this person who leads the worship in church singing at the top of her voice?

This is the work of a loving God! This is the work of a powerful Spirit! This is the work of a Master Potter!

In his book 'George Müller of Bristol', A. T. Pierson writes: "We cannot make God essentially any more glorious, for He is infinitely perfect; but we can help men to see what a glorious God He is, and thus come into that holy partnership with the Spirit of God whose office it is to take the things of Christ and show them unto men, and so glorify Christ." What better way to glorify God to others than to be perceptibly transformed by the power of the Holy Spirit from one filled with the spirit of darkness to one filled with the spirit of light.

We must exercise our spiritual senses if we are to discern things spiritual. There is a clear vision for God's goodness, and there is a dull eye that sees little to be thankful for; there is a tender conscience, and there is a moral sense that grows less and less sensitive to evil; there is an obedience to the Spirit's rebuke which leads to immediate confession and increases strength

for every new conflict. Mr. Müller cultivated habits of life which made his whole nature more and more open to divine impression, and so his sense of God became more and more keen and constant...As he saw divine things

more clearly and felt their supreme importance, he became engrossed in the magnifying of them before men; and this is glorifying God.

A. T. Pierson

The Potter's House

In case you have fallen by the wayside of life

Dreams and visions shattered, you're all broken inside

You don't have to stay in the shape that you're in

The Potter wants to put you back together again

O, the Potter wants to put you back together again

In case your situation has turned upside down

And all that you've accomplished is now in the ground

You don't have to stay in the shape that you're in

The Potter wants to put you back together again

O, the Potter wants to put you back together again

You – who are broken, step by the Potter's house

You – who need mending, step by the Potter's house

Give Him the fragments of your broken life, my friend

The Potter wants to put you back together again

O, the Potter wants to put you back together again

You – who are broken, step by the Potter's house

You – who need mending, step by the Potter's house

If your heart needs mending, step by Jesus' house
Give Him the fragments of your broken life,
The Potter wants to put you back together again

You'll find joy – in the Potter's house
He'll give you joy

You'll find peace – in the Potter's house
I know there's peace in the Potter's house (for the riven soul)

You'll find love – in the Potter's house
If you're looking for love – the Potter has it

And there's salvation – in the Potter's house

God will change your life
If you need healing for your body – you'll find it

Thank God – there's deliverance! For any kind of habit

You'll find everything you need, in the Potter's house

You'll find happiness there

Because, the Potter wants to put you back together again

O, the Potter wants to put you back together again.

Sung by Tramaine Hawkins
Great Women of Gospel, EMI Gospel

**But the pot he was shaping from the clay
was marred in his hands; so the potter
formed it into another pot, shaping it
as seemed best to him.**

Jeremiah 18:4

I Am a New Creation

I am a new creation,
no more in condemnation,
here in the grace of God I stand.

My heart is overflowing,
my love just keeps on growing,
here in the grace of God I stand.

And I will praise You, Lord,
yes I will praise You, Lord,
and I will sing of all that You have done.

A joy that knows no limit,
a lightness in my spirit,
here in the grace of God I stand.

Dave Bilbrough

**Therefore, if anyone is in Christ, he is a new creation;
the old has gone, the new has come!**

2 Corinthians 5:17

Joy is peace dancing.
Peace is joy resting.

Jim Graham

Within each one of us there is a God-shaped vacuum that only God can fill.

Pascal

Things turn out best for the people who make the best out of the way things turn out.

Art Linkletter

Never be ashamed of laughter that is too loud
or singing that is too joyful.

Anon

I have come that they may have life,
and have it to the full.

John 10:10

Grace – The unconditional and undeserved love of God which, if we recognise and accept it, will work upon us from the inside and gradually make us into better people.

Invictus

By William Ernest Henley

Out of the night that covers me,

Black as the pit from pole to pole,

I thank whatever gods may be

For my unconquerable soul.

In the fell clutch of circumstance

I have not winced nor cried aloud.

Under the bludgeonings of chance

My head is bloody, but unbowed.

Beyond this place of wrath and tears
Looms but the Horror of the shade,
And yet the menace of the years
Finds and shall find me unafraid.

It matters not how strait the gate,
How charged with punishment the scroll,
I am the master of my fate,
I am the captain of my soul.

www.ingramcontent.com/pod-product-compliance
Lightning Source LLC
Chambersburg PA
CBHW070457170726
48291CB00008B/2546